*Jackie,
Love endures every goodbye*

First Class Farewell

by AJ Harmon

http://www.firstclassnovels.com

First Print Edition, November 2013

Copyright 2013 by ABCs Legacy, LLC

All rights reserved. This book may not be reproduced in any form, in whole or in part, without written permission from the author.

Dedication

As this series comes to an end, I have so many people who have made a huge impact in my life, especially over this past year. To my family, first and foremost, I am so grateful for your love and support. To my team that makes it possible for me to publish my stories, I am in your debt for your skill and service. To my friends that have been so supportive I say Thank you. Your encouragement is much appreciated.

To the many wonderful people who have bought my books – thank you! Thank you for your kind reviews, your interaction with me through Facebook and emails. You have made this past year more than I had ever dreamed of. Thank you! Thank you! Thank you!

Table of Contents

CHAPTER

1. Peter & Maureen	1
2. Matt & Janie	11
3. Mark & Katy	27
4. Andrew & Rory	31
5. David & Lindsey	37
6. Ben & Sophia	45
7. Paul & Nic	55
8. Tim & Beth	63
9. The Obituary	71
10. Goodbye	83
11. The Wake	95
12. Ghosts	109
13. Awakening	117
14. Prodding	129
15. Pedicures… & More Prodding	141
16. Dinner	153
17. Surprises	161
18. Maternal Instinct	169
19. Realization	177
20. Possibility	191
21. Clarity	203
22. Desire	217
EPILOGUE	229
ABOUT THE AUTHOR	233

1.

Peter & Maureen

Since the day that Peter Lathem retired, he'd made golfing his hobby of choice. In good weather he played at his favorite golf course with three of his buddies. If the weather was not so good, he headed to the Chelsea Piers driving range and hit balls until his bucket was empty and his back ached. Today, being an almost perfect spring morning, Peter met his friends for coffee at the small diner a couple of blocks from his home and then they drove to New Jersey and the country club where they would spend several hours arguing over handicaps and the most recent Yankees game.

Peter, a die-hard Yankees fan, could not accept anyone speaking ill of his beloved team. His friends liked to push his buttons and could usually get him so riled that he'd throw a club, or two, by the end of eighteen holes. In fact, they took it as a challenge to up the number of clubs to three. So far, however, they'd failed.

With Peter out of the house on the crisp Thursday morning, Maureen loaded the dishwasher with the breakfast dishes, stripped her bed of the linens in preparation for the housekeeper to remake, and put a load of laundry in the washer. By nine o'clock she was ready to leave the house for the grocery store to shop for the weekly Sunday dinner.

As a young mother, Maureen had been determined to have all evening meals together as a family; sitting around the table sharing the events of the day. As her boys aged and extra-curricular activities took them away from the family home more and more, and eventually off to college, the mandatory weekly Sunday dinner was born.

The Lathems were devout in their religion and Sunday was dedicated to God and family. As children, Mass was not optional, and as adults, most of them still attended the family parish regularly. Dinner came after Mass and as her sons married and began having families of their own, the dinners became more important to her. It was imperative that the cousins grew up together; getting to know each other and playing together; becoming friends. Not only had she replaced the dining table with a much larger one, there was now a grandchildren's table, a sight that filled her heart with more love than she ever thought one woman could possess. The sight and sounds of them eating and playing filled her with joy.

Even though each son had married their perfect partner, and all willing to contribute to the family meal, Maureen had kept control of the protein and the dessert and then assigned sides among the daughters-in-law. Rory always brought the wine. Even with a celebrated chef in the family, Maureen stuck with the tradition she had started fifty years before and shopped and cooked each week for the family get-together. With her shopping list in hand, and Ray waiting for her at the curb, Maureen locked the door behind her and took the steps one at a time down to the sidewalk.

Ray was Matt's - Maureen's eldest son - longtime driver and most trusted employee. Actually, he was considered part of the family. He often celebrated holidays and birthdays with the Lathems and occasionally accompanied Matt and his family to their vacation home in the Bahamas. Now that Matt was practically retired,

Ray took care of Peter and Maureen more and more, driving them anytime they left the city and every Tuesday and Thursday when Maureen did her grocery shopping. Ray took her hand and helped her into the back seat of the black BMW and then drove to the market.

Although he would never admit it, Ray enjoyed taking Maureen to the store. He pushed the cart as the two of them discussed anything and everything; the ongoing war in the Middle East, the weather, Ray's two beautiful daughters who were now in college, the price of gas, and hundreds of other topics. As Maureen paid for her groceries, Ray would load them into the cart and then into the trunk of the car and, once again, help Maureen into the car and drive her home. Once there, he made sure to see her inside and settled before unloading the car and quite often helping her put the groceries away in the pantry and refrigerator. Then, Maureen would make them both lunch before it was time for Ray to pick up one of the children, Ella, Christopher, Alex, or all of them, and return to the office or Matt's apartment.

As Matt had scaled back in his official duties as CEO and President of MEL Holdings, the demand on Ray's time also decreased, but Matt had made sure his salary had increased. Ray had protested but to no avail. He was employed by the most generous man he'd ever known and treasured his relationship with the Lathem family. It wasn't just a job. He loved them all.

Maureen had made BLT sandwiches for lunch and with them eaten and the kitchen tidied, Ray kissed her on the cheek and left for St. Luke's where the children were at school. It was already after two and they would be dismissed at three o'clock. There wasn't enough time to do anything else, so while he waited he hoped one of his daughters would answer their cell phones when he called.

*****

Peter had never been an exceptional golfer but that didn't deter his love for the game. At eighty years old, he didn't have the swing of his younger days, but he didn't mind. Being out in the fresh air with his friends was what it was all about now. Some days, he let the others keep score because he didn't care how many strokes he took. He was glad to still be alive and able to walk the course, although he rarely did. That's what the golf carts were for, after all.

Sitting in the club and eating his salad with blackened salmon he enjoyed the company of his dear friends. They'd all worked together in the insurance business for many, many years. More years than Peter liked to think about. They'd remained friends after one by one they'd retired. Herb and Vince were now widowers and Ed's wife had been placed in a nursing home after falling and breaking her hip. Sadly, it didn't look like she would ever return home. Not only did Peter need them, but they needed him, too, and they each looked forward to their time together. Who knew how long they would all be around?

Loading all the golf bags in the back of the car, they drove back to Manhattan through the Holland Tunnel and up to the diner where they'd met earlier in the day. After unloading the clubs, they said goodbye and headed in four different directions, Peter going home to his wife.

*****

Four stories and four bathrooms made it very difficult for Maureen to do all the cleaning in her home. As a young mother she had prided herself on her house always being in tip-top condition and at first, she had balked of the idea of a housekeeper coming in twice a week to clean. It was an embarrassment to her to admit she could no longer scrub the bathtub or clean the floor behind the toilet. Liko had been a blessing, though. She was at Matt and Janie's home two days a week, Mark and Katy's one day a week, and Maureen's the other two. Matt believed that once you found someone you trusted and who exceeded all expectations, you made sure you treated them well, paid them what they were worth and made sure they had no reason to ever leave your employ. Liko fit into this category. She'd worked for the Lathems for years and loved the family.

As Maureen headed upstairs to her bedroom, she found Liko adding the pillows to the re-made bed.

"Thank you, Liko," Maureen smiled. "There are some things that I just can't do anymore." She sat in the armchair under the window and removed her shoes. "You know you're getting old when just going to the market should be rewarded with a nap."

"That's a good idea," agreed Liko. "You do look tired."

"I think I've been tired all year," she chuckled.

Liko helped Maureen to the bed and then pulled a light blanket from the chest at the foot of the bed and covered her.

"Peter should be home soon and he'll want an afternoon snack. Don't let me sleep too long."

"I can fix him a little something," Liko offered. "You just rest."

Maureen closed her eyes and Liko tiptoed from the room, closing the door behind her. When Peter arrived home just a short time later, Liko made him a snack of vegetables and crackers, even though he asked for a chocolate shake and a donut. She knew Maureen tried to keep him on a balanced diet.

"But I had salad for lunch," he whined like a child. "I deserve a donut."

Liko grinned and pulled a chocolate candy bar from the back of the pantry. "Eat your vegetables and I'll let you have this when you're done."

"I'm not a child," Peter frowned, but began munching on his baby carrots and celery sticks. Placing the chocolate on the table next to him, Liko handed him the remote to the television and returned to cleaning the house.

*****

With Ella and Christopher safely returned home after school, and his services not required for the rest of the day, Ray grabbed the car vac and some leather cleaning wipes and headed to the underground garage to spruce up the car. With the inside spotless, he popped open the trunk to give it the once over and discovered two jars of roasted red peppers hidden from view. *Damn!* he thought. They must have escaped from Maureen's grocery bags. Ray slipped behind the wheel and began the journey uptown.

Peter had snuck into the bedroom to check on Maureen. She had complained of a slight headache so he'd checked the cabinet in the bathroom for a pain reliever.

"I need aspirin," she'd whispered. "The other stuff

doesn't do a thing."

But there wasn't any in the cupboard. "I have everything else but no aspirin," he frowned. Looking back at his wife, he could see her face scrunched in pain. "I'll walk to the corner market. They should have some." Peter quickly slipped on some shoes, grabbed his wallet and kissed his wife on the forehead. "Be back in a flash."

Maureen grinned. "You haven't *flashed* in a long time."

Peter kissed her again and closed the bedroom door behind him and hurried down the stairs. As he opened the front door, Ray pulled into the empty parking space in front of the house next door. He stepped onto the sidewalk and Peter could see two jars in his hands.

"Are you delivering now?" Peter chuckled.

Ray shook his head and smiled. "I guess they rolled out of the grocery bags in the trunk."

"Can you put them inside? I need to get to the market to buy some aspirin. Maureen isn't feeling well."

"Let me take you," Ray offered. "Just let me run these downstairs."

Peter stepped aside and Ray ran inside and was back out in less than a minute. "Let's go."

The two men rode the three blocks to the corner market that the Lathems visited in emergencies. It didn't sell much more than beer, cigarettes and lottery tickets, but Peter was hopeful he would find at least a small bottle of aspirin. There also wasn't any parking so Ray dropped

Peter off at the front door and said he'd drive around the block and pick him up. Peter thanked him and strode inside the open door.

As Ray pulled back in front after taking a few minutes to maneuver the car around the block, his heart stopped as he peered through the large glass window. Throwing the car into park, he ripped off his seat belt and ran for Peter who was staring at a thug with a gun.

*****

The cool wash cloth was helping. Maureen's eyes could focus when her eyelids fluttered open and the sickly feeling had subsided. Taking a deep breath, she attempted to sit up as there came a knock on the bedroom door.

"Mrs. Lathem?" called Liko.

"Come in," she replied.

The doorknob turned and Liko stepped into the room. "Mrs. Lathem? I need you to come downstairs with me. There's someone here to see you."

"Who?" Maureen asked.

"Please? Come with me." Liko had walked around to help Maureen up and the two women walked down the flight of stairs to the front door. There stood two policemen.

"Mrs. Lathem?" one of them asked.

"Yes?" Maureen answered.

"May we come in, please?"

2.

Matt & Janie

As he stood at the edge of the bed and glanced at the clock, 5:47, his eyes drifted to the woman still sleeping peacefully in his bed. Her lips were slightly parted and he could hear her deep breaths. Her bare shoulder peeked out from under the sheet and the smooth pale skin called to him like a siren. He should get dressed and go and work out in the gym, but the knowledge that a beautiful woman lay naked in his bed was too much for his waning resolve and he lifted the blankets and slid in behind her, nuzzling her neck, kissing that shoulder, and his hand caressing the ass that cradled his bulging erection.

Matt should let her sleep. After all, he'd kept her up until midnight making love to her before they drifted off to sleep entwined in each other's arms. But even after twelve years he couldn't get enough of her. Janie was the light and love of his life. His existence was without meaning unless she was by his side.

"Morning," she mumbled as she grabbed his wandering hand and placed it on her breast.

"Good morning to you," Matt breathed into her shoulder.

Janie rolled onto her back and Matt kissed her passionately as he pulled himself up and hovered over her before settling in between her legs.

"How much time do we have?" she asked sleepily.

"Enough," he grinned and kissed her again.

Janie ran her hands through his dark hair, now with a smattering of grey at his temples. "I love you," she smiled.

Matt kissed her again and entered her slowly, the love he felt for his wife pouring from every pore as he worshipped her with his body. Janie arched her back and closed her eyes as every one of her senses drowned in the union of their bodies…their hearts…their minds and their souls.

The sensual thrusts turned more urgent and Matt's rhythm built as their bodies craved a blissful release until they heard the doorknob twist and both gasped in horror. Matt collapsed on his wife, shielding her with his body and desperately trying to find the sheet to cover his ass before one of their children wandered into their bedroom. Just as Janie was able to grab the corner of the Egyptian cotton, the door flung open and a sleepy eight year old toddled toward the bed.

"Mom? Can we have waffles for breakfast?"

Matt skillfully covered their entangled limbs with the sheet and Janie turned her head and faced the opposite direction, knowing she could not speak to her son with her husband still inside her, embarrassment all too apparent.

"Hey bud," Matt grinned. "You're up early. Why don't you go and get dressed and Mom will make you waffles in just a few minutes. Is Ella still asleep?"

"I dunno," Christopher yawned.

"Okay, well, Mom and I will get up it just a minute, 'k?"

"Okay. What are you guys doing? Why are you lying on Mom?"

"She was cold. I'm warming her up. Go get dressed."

Christopher accepted his father's answer without question and wandered back out and shut the door behind him. Matt burst out laughing.

"That was not funny," Janie muttered. "I knew this day would come, but…"

"But nothing!" Matt grinned. "He suspects nothing. He's just as innocent as before he walked in. Now, where were we?"

*****

While there was never *any* doubt that Matt was Christopher's father, after eating two Belgian waffles, three strips of bacon and two sausage patties, Janie shook her head as Christopher asked for the waffle that she was plating for Matt. At eight years old, he could *almost* out-eat his father.

"Three?" Janie asked. "Are you hungry?"

"Yeah. Well, *I'm* not, but my muscles are," he replied.

"Your muscles are hungry?" Matt grinned and patiently waited for his breakfast.

"I'm growing like a weed according to Grandpa and

my muscles are always hungry. I think that's why I'm getting so strong," he said matter-of-factly as he took a large bite, syrup dripping onto his chin.

Janie and Matt looked at each other and smiled. Ella rolled her eyes.

"Waffles will make you fat," she sighed. "I wish I could eat them but I can't risk it."

"What?" Matt exclaimed. "You are not fat! Where on earth would you get that idea?"

"I didn't say I was fat, Dad. I said that waffles will make me fat if I eat them. I have to avoid carbs."

"You're ten!" Janie was horrified. "You can eat waffles! Is that why you don't want any?"

"I'm almost eleven," she glared. "And Belinda was telling us all about the dangers of carbs yesterday at lunch. She said that I shouldn't eat bread or potatoes or rice, and definitely no sugar. Her mother is having some kind of thing where the doctor is going to remove the carbs from her body, so she told Belinda that is was much easier not to eat them in the first place."

Matt's mouth dropped open in disgust. "You are *not* fat and you will not *get* fat if you eat a waffle. Your mother does not feed you food that will make you gain weight. We eat a balanced diet that includes carbs *and* sugar! Belinda's mother needs to take some parenting classes."

"Honey," Janie said to her daughter when she didn't respond to her father's comments. "You are beautiful and healthy. You take dance classes and karate and play soccer. In order to do those things your body must have carbs. They are what produce the energy for you to dance and run and play. If you stop eating them, you won't be able to do all the things you love. Do you not want to dance anymore?"

"I do want to dance!"

"Then you're body demands carbs and protein. Tell you what. After school today, I'll show you all the stuff I have on fitness and how to maintain your body and be healthy. And then you can tell Belinda to…"

"What a great idea!" Janie cut off Matt before he said something about Ella's friend. "What do you think, Ella?"

She nodded. "It sounds interesting. Maybe I could invite Belinda over some time and you could tell her, too."

"Sure," Matt smiled. "Now eat a waffle!"

The sound of Ray whistling sent Christopher jumping off his stool and running through the kitchen. "Ray!" he exclaimed and grabbed his hand and dragged him to an empty stool at the island in the large kitchen. "Mom's making waffles. Want some?"

Ray grinned as Janie filled a mug with coffee and added a dash of cream and set it in front of their good friend.

"Already had a bagel, but thanks," he replied and ruffled Christopher's hair.

"Are you sure?" Janie asked. "There's plenty."

"Well, I wouldn't want it to go to waste," he grinned.

And he didn't. With everyone having eaten, even Ella, the kids were sent to brush their teeth and then Ray would take them to school, as usual. As he'd said many times before, chauffeuring the children was the favorite part of his day. His two daughters were grown and at college, and even though he hadn't seen much of them during their teen years after his ex-wife had moved to Detroit, there was a feeling of melancholy of not having young children anymore. Ella and Christopher filled that void and he loved them like his own…and they loved him. Actually, they adored him. Ella still kissed him goodbye when she got out of the car at school, something she didn't even do to her parents anymore. And while Ray would never admit it to Matt, his employer, he'd do this job for free. The Lathems were his family and he loved them all and took great care and pride in serving them to the best of his abilities.

He left about ten minutes before the kids were ready to go and pull the car in front of the apartment building. After kissing their mother, the children were escorted by their father down the elevator, through the lobby and to the waiting car at the curb. There was nobody else that he trusted the care of his children to more than Ray. He waved as they pulled into traffic and headed to Ben and Sophia's apartment to pick up Alex on the way, and then they would drive uptown to St. Luke's. With a grin, Matt returned to his wife.

*****

As Matt walked back into his apartment, he smiled at the thought of it being Thursday. How his life had changed over the past few years. Now retired, with the exception of a few meetings here and there, his life was his family, and surprising even himself, he couldn't have been happier. He acknowledged his fortunate circumstances. Not marrying Janie until he was forty had allowed him to build his empire without ever sacrificing time with her and the children they had brought into the world together. He had begun scaling back his hours the day they returned from their honeymoon, knowing he would much prefer to spend his days with his wife than behind his desk at his office. And now he rarely went to the office as his company was being run by his brother, Ben, and when it was time for him to begin his exit, Tyler and Derek were in the wings waiting for their turn to helm the ship. Matt and Mark's step-sons were intelligent and shrewd businessmen. They had been mentored by the best in the business and had blossomed under their tutelage.

"What are you smiling at?" Janie asked as Matt entered the kitchen where Janie was finishing cleaning up from breakfast.

"It's Thursday and I'm here with you," he grinned and whirled her around in a circle. "And the kids are at school!"

"I have to go to the animal shelter today. I promised to help out with the fundraiser preparations. I'll only be gone for a couple of hours, though. Is there something that can keep you busy 'til I get back?"

Matt frowned. "I suppose," he pouted.

Janie laughed. "Tell you what. Why don't you meet me for lunch at the Thai place and then we can walk home together. Maybe you can get a little action before the kids come home," she winked.

"You know we don't have to make love in order for me to want to spend time with you," he said as he ran his fingers through her hair and pulled her lips to his. "I will even go shopping with you if that's what you want to do."

"I would never be so cruel," she laughed. "Besides, it's been a while since we *enjoyed* the desk."

"I do love that desk," he grinned, wiggling his eyebrows. "And I love it when you're naked on that desk."

"Well, let me get to the shelter and get the stuff done there and then we can think about the desk."

Matt gave her a kiss on the tip on her nose and released her from his hold. "I'm the luckiest man in the world, you know that?"

"Yes, I do," she replied as she gathered her purse and jacket, ready for her morning of volunteering.

After Janie had left, Matt wandered through to the gym and used the couple of hours to work off his waffles, the conversation with his daughter at breakfast replaying in his head. The thought of her having any issues with her body at the ripe old age of ten made him sick. The day she'd been born was the day he'd sworn to protect her from the world and so far he'd been able to live up to that promise, but this was something for which he was ill-prepared.

Ella was the mini version of Janie. She had big blue eyes that screamed of innocence. Her hair was a medium shade of brown with little golden highlights that glistened in the sun. She would always be his baby and he would fight demons to protect her. He would walk on fire for her and the idea that she was already being brainwashed into what society's notion of what beauty was scared him to death. Matt's second wife had been vain and shallow and pre-occupied with size and the BMI chart. It drove him crazy. What he loved most about Janie was that she was who she was...there was no pretending to be something she wasn't. It was true she'd gained some weight over the past couple of years. Hitting menopause had been hard on her, but if anything, Matt loved her more. She was soft and sweet and the size of her jeans meant nothing to him. She was his eternal love. Somehow he needed to make Ella understand that weight was just a number...it didn't determine who she was.

As he ran on the treadmill and worked out on the weight machine, he wondered if it would help to have Ella see a therapist, but as quickly as the thought came, it was replaced by a better one.

"I'll have Mom talk to her," he said to himself as he headed for the shower. "Nobody tells it like it is better than Mom!"

*****

At precisely noon, Matt met Janie in front of their favorite Thai restaurant just a few blocks from their apartment. Like newlyweds, they sat side by side, fingers entwined as they ordered lunch and sipped their drinks, Janie a lemonade and Matt an iced tea.

"So tell me all about your morning," she asked.

"I just hit the gym," Matt shrugged. "My favorite thing to do wasn't there," he grinned.

"I should hit the treadmill this afternoon," Janie sighed.

"Not on my account," he replied as he caressed her thigh. "You're perfect."

"That's sweet," Janie smiled, "but you lie," she chuckled.

"I do not! You wound me with that accusation. You *are* perfect and I can't imagine loving you more."

Janie kissed him on the cheek.

"What exciting things did you do today?" he asked.

"Centerpieces," she said. "Each table is going to have the story of one of the rescued animals, so all the photos needed to be trimmed and put into frames. It was very glamorous work," she grinned.

The annual humane society benefit gala was very important to Janie and Matt. Just three days after they'd first met, he'd taken her to the lavish fundraiser that his company donated large amounts of money to every year. Once married and living in New York City, Janie had become very involved with the organization and she and Matt attended the function each year. Now just three weeks away, she was spending several hours a week in preparation, as she was on the three-woman planning committee made up of volunteers to assist the director in his quest to outdo the past years' donations. She was committed to the cause and enjoyed directing her attention to it when the children were in school.

The waitress delivered their food and with gusto, they each devoured the noodles placed before them.

"Sticky rice and mangoes?" Matt asked Janie as they finished their entrees.

Janie was non-committal in her response.

"You're gonna need your carbs when we get home," he winked.

"Okay, then," she laughed.

*****

The view from their bedroom window was glorious. With sweat dripping from their joined bodies, Janie's legs still wrapped around her husband's waist, she leaned back on the desk and gazed at Lady Liberty.

"I'm so glad we didn't move our bedroom when we remodeled. I can't imagine not having this view."

"Me either," Matt agreed, although he was looking at his wife's breasts as he spoke.

Janie giggled and threw her arms around his neck and hugged him tightly. "We'd better get dressed. The kids will be here shortly and I don't think you could talk your way out this," she laughed.

With a quick kiss on her forehead, Matt released her and helped her off the desk and into the sprawling marble bathroom. Cleaned up and dressed, they walked hand in hand through to the kitchen where Janie began making a batch of oatmeal cookies in preparation for an afterschool snack for her kids, although she knew Matt would eat most of them.

It wasn't long before the sounds of backpacks being dropped on the floor and three identifiable voices were heard and the kitchen once again became the heart of their home. Ray declined the offer of cookies and milk and headed down to the garage to clean the car. Both children said goodbye to him and then climbed up to the island and impatiently waited for their mother to retrieve the first batch from the oven.

With glasses of milk for Ella and Christopher and coffee for Matt, the three of them devoured the first plate of twelve cookies in less than two minutes. Janie just smiled as she continued to drop scoops of cookie dough onto the baking sheets.

The sound of the front door closing had all eyes looking up as Adam sauntered into the kitchen.

"I see I arrived at the perfect moment," he grinned and hugged his mom.

"Adam! What a terrific surprise. I thought you'd be working," she said as she grabbed a glass from the cupboard. Pouring him some milk, she put the glass on the island in front of the empty stool.

"I took the afternoon off."

His statement took Matt by surprise. His stepson was one of the hardest working men he knew. As a pediatrician with a booming practice, time off was one thing Adam didn't do.

"And you came here?" Janie asked.

"To see you guys," he grinned at Ella and Christopher

and gave them both a hug.

"Can you stay for dinner?" Janie was hopeful to have some time with her son.

"Nah," Adam shook his head. "I promised Shelby I'd help her study. She has exams starting on Monday."

And there it is, Matt thought. Over the past few years, Matt had wondered what Adam and Shelby's relationship was. Yes, they were basically family, although not related in any way. Shelby was a very close friend of Katy's, Matt's sister-in-law. In fact, she was more like a surrogate daughter. And while Matt considered Adam his son, they were not biologically related at all. At family gatherings, Adam and Shelby seemed to spend a lot of time together, but there had never been anything out of the ordinary...never any signs that they were anything more than friends. Matt, however, wondered if he was just missing something. Now to hear that Adam would take time off work to help her study had him questioning even more.

"This is it, right?" Matt asked. "She graduates next month?"

"Yep. Just has to get through finals and she's all done with school. Then comes the hard part," Adam nodded.

"What could be harder than school?" Ella asked.

"When you want to be a doctor, you have to go to school for a long time and then you have work in a hospital and that's usually harder than school," Adam told his little sister.

"You don't work in a hospital," Christopher noted.

"Well, not very often," Adam agreed. "But I did until just a couple of years ago. And it was hard work."

"Is Shelby going to be a doctor like you? Will she be our doctor, too?" Ella asked.

Adam shook his head. "Nope. I'm your pediatrician and you get to come and see me until you go to college. Shelby is going to be another kind of doctor."

Ella and Christopher took another cookie leaving Janie an opportunity to talk to her son. "So where's Shelby then?"

"She had lunch with some friends. I'm going to meet up with her in a just a bit but I had a few minutes to kill so I figured I'd swing by and say hi."

"Well, I'm glad you did," Janie smiled. "If only Tyler were here," she sighed.

"He's in Berlin 'til Saturday," Adam informed his parents. "He said he'd be back for Sunday dinner."

Adam turned his attention to his younger siblings. At first, it had been strange for him to have a younger brother and sister. After all, he'd been in his mid-twenties when they'd been born. Now, however, he couldn't imagine life without them. He adored them and they, in turn, adored him. He was their big brother, their pediatrician, and he loved them dearly.

After almost thirty minutes of chatting with his family, Adam said his goodbyes and the children went to the family room with their father to do their homework. That left Janie to tidy up the kitchen and begin preparing dinner. As she unloaded the dishwasher, and absent-mindedly opened drawers and cupboards putting things away, her mind drifted over the past few years and the happiness she felt.

Still madly in love with her husband, Janie thanked God every day for meeting him in the Portland airport all those years ago. Their life had been blessed with two beautiful and healthy children, a lovely home, and a comfortable life. She acknowledged her blessings and was grateful for them.

As she peeled potatoes for dinner, Janie couldn't help but smile. Life was simply marvelous. The telephone rang and interrupted her thoughts. Wiping her hands on a tea towel, she smiled as she saw her in-law's name appear on the Caller I.D.

"Hello."

"Janie?"

"Oh, Liko. Hello."

But as she heard the words come through the phone, the smile disappeared from her face and she suddenly felt ill.

"Matt!" she screamed, with her hand covering the phone. "God, no!" she cried. "Matt!"

3.

Mark & Katy

Typically, Thursdays were Katy's favorite day of the week. Monday was the day Mark spent at the office. Tuesdays and Wednesdays were the days that Katy volunteered at the women's shelter. But Thursday was the day that began the long weekend that she fiercely protected as family time. Whether it was just her and Mark, or with Derek, or Shelby, or the whole family, Katy loved the promise of Thursdays and the weekend.

"You're married to an old man," Mark chuckled as he swung his legs over the side of the bed and sat up. "I sound like a bowl of Rice Krispies when I move."

"I'll take some snap, crackle and pop," Katy grinned. "A hot shower will warm up those joints. I'll even join you."

"Well, that's an offer I'm not going to refuse," Mark replied. "Get your ass out of bed and go and start the water then, woman!"

Katy threw her head back and laughed loudly. "If you want me to do your bidding, that's definitely the *wrong* way to go about it."

Mark grinned. "How about this then? Once the water is warm and my muscles are loosened, I'll make you scream with pleasure," he said with a low growl.

"That, my dear husband, will get me out of bed and starting the shower," she giggled as she leapt from the bed and ran to the bathroom.

*****

Even though they had recently celebrated their eighth wedding anniversary, Mark and Katy still acted like newlyweds. They held hands constantly and Mark was not afraid to show public displays of affection with his wife. They were very much in love and deeply committed to one another and they still enjoyed spending time together. The day's itinerary confirmed that fact.

After a bowl of cereal and a piece of whole wheat toast, they loaded a picnic basket into the trunk of their car, strapped their bikes onto the roof rack and left the city for a bike trail in Connecticut. The drive took only about an hour and a half and then they had helmets on and they were off. The morning air was still a tad cool but the exercise put color in their cheeks as they climbed hills and whizzed down the other side. After a couple of hours of wondrous fun, they arrived back at the car. With a blanket and their lunch, under a tall tree made a perfect spot for a cozy picnic.

Bottles of cold water provided instant relief for their parched throats and with her legs crossed, Katy proceeded to serve lunch. Broccoli salad and hummus with pita chips were first out of the basket, followed by croissants filled with creamy chicken salad. Mark uncorked the bottle of Pino Grigio and Katy unwrapped the glasses wrapped in linen napkins for their protection.

As they ate, they recalled their favorite parts of the trail they'd just ridden and reviewed the map and decided on the trail they would take after lunch. They'd picked the hardest one for their first ride and would take on one not nearly as difficult for their afternoon exercise before heading back to the city and dinner at The Bourbon.

"You can go in front this time," Mark said as he scooped a blob of the smooth hummus onto a chip.

"Okay," she replied.

"I want to watch your ass," he grinned and winked.

Katy smiled and kissed the tip of his nose. She poured some more wine in their glasses and then re-corked the bottle and laid it in the bottom of the wicker basket. "You can watch my ass anytime."

"I know," Mark said. "And I do."

Katy chuckled and continued repacking the basket. Mark's cell phone rang and he frowned as he read the caller's name.

"I'll try to make it brief," he said as he answered. Saying hello to Ryan, the company's CFO, Mark scrambled to his feet and wandered off leaving Katy to lie back on the blanket and watch the leaves rustle in the slight breeze overhead. She closed her eyes, her husband's faint voice and the sound of the trees relaxing her.

When she reopened her eyes, Mark was snuggled next to her, breathing softly. She'd fallen asleep...and so had he. The wine and the energetic bike ride had allowed her to drift off without her even realizing it. Katy watched the fluffy white clouds in the sky as they drifted slowly, changing shape. *So much for another ride,* she smiled, although it had been a wonderful way to spend the afternoon, enjoying the sun and the trees.

She glanced at her watch and was shocked to see that she'd slept for an hour, but she didn't move. She remained in the safety and comfort of her husband's arms and enjoyed the moment.

On the ride back to the city, thirty minutes later, Mark had admitted that she'd looked so peaceful when he returned to her after finishing his phone call that he didn't have the heart to wake her, although he never imagined that he'd fall asleep, too.

"It's a sign of old age," he muttered.

Katy laughed. They were in the throes of middle age, of that she couldn't deny. But they were young middle-aged, if there were such a thing. She refused to grow old before her time. Just as she was about to inform her husband that they still had many, *many* years before they reached the age of *old*, Mark's phone starting buzzing again. He pulled it from the console of the car and read Matt's name. He handed Katy the phone and she answered the call.

"Hey, Matt," she smiled as she answered. "He's driving but I can put you on speaker."

Mark stopped the car at the red light after turning off the Henry Hudson Parkway. He watched Katy's expression change, and when she said, "we'll be right there," his heart stopped for a moment. This wasn't going to be good.

4.

Andrew & Rory

They'd met at a party, both invited by a mutual friend. They'd attended the same university in Seattle but didn't meet until a month before graduation. It wasn't love at first sight. In fact, after that night, they didn't see each other again for five years, when once again, they were both invited to a party by a mutual friend, this time in New York City.

Andrew was establishing himself as a successful stock broker, working for a major powerhouse in the business. Rory, now an attorney, left the west coast and the family who no longer accepted him for being an openly gay man, and moved as far away as possible. He'd hoped New York would be a good fit and after taking another bar prep course, and another bar exam, he found himself working in a small law firm and building his reputation as an excellent attorney.

The party was for a mutual friend who had recently been declared cancer free and was throwing a bash that rivalled that of New Years' Eve. Andrew and Rory were surprised to come face to face at the bar. They ended up spending most of the night talking and getting to know each other and as the saying goes, the rest was history. Now, well over twenty years later, they were married with two children and praying a third would grace their family soon.

"There is no way in hell you are leaving the house dressed like that!" Rory exclaimed as Isabelle arrived for breakfast.

"What's wrong with it?" she asked.

Andrew sighed, knowing that arguing with their eight year old daughter was an uphill battle and neither side ever won. "Father James will not allow the uniform to be…to be changed."

Isabelle had somehow shortened her pleated grey skirt, and she hadn't done it well, but Andrew had to give her an A for effort.

"What did you do?" Rory asked and lifted the hem to find an ugly mess of masking tape barely holding the new hem in place. "Oh, no!" he shook his head. "It's all coming off. And undo that ridiculous knot in your shirt."

"But all the girls do it," she whined.

"All the girls where?" Andrew asked.

"On TV," she shrugged.

"Good grief," Rory muttered. "Masking tape off! Shirt untied and tucked in, and take the sneakers off and put on your black shoes."

"Fine!" she pouted. "When can I start wearing makeup?"

Andrew ran his hand through his hair and leaned back in his chair. "You are a beautiful girl. You don't need to muddy up your face with that junk."

"You sound just like Grandma," she sighed.

"Oh God," Andrew muttered.

At that moment, Joseph decided he didn't want the cereal on the table and threw it on the floor. Rory slid from his chair and knelt in front of their five year old son and tenderly took his hand and caressed his arm. Massage always helped Joseph to calm down. He rarely spoke but managed to make his feelings known. Rory and Tilly, their nanny, were the only ones that were able to soothe him once a tantrum began. The two fathers had become experts on autism and Joseph had in fact blossomed in their home.

Joseph had come to the Lathem-Jeffers home when he was eighteen months old. A ward of the state, his parents had signed away all parental rights when they were unable to control his outbursts and tantrums. He'd been in foster care for a little over three months when Rory heard about him at a luncheon when he overheard another attorney talking about the sad situation. Without telling Andrew, he'd contacted the Department of Child Services and had even questioned them on the possibility of adoption. Then, tactfully and cautiously, he'd broached the subject with Andrew one evening when the conversation had drifted to adding another child to their family. As expected, Andrew was wary of taking on a child with such special needs, but Rory had pleaded the case well, being an exceptional litigator.

"The boy needs love and we have that in abundance. He needs security and we can offer that, too. He needs someone with resources to secure the best therapists and schools available and we can also do that. We have all he needs. I think we should meet him and see how it goes."

And so they did. It took almost an hour before Joseph would approach them, but after he had, he grabbed onto Rory's leg and refused to let go. There was no way Andrew could deny the bond between father and son that was already forming. It only took a couple of weeks before Joseph was placed with his new family, as they had already completed the foster parent licensing process before they adopted Isabelle. But it took several weeks before Joseph warmed up to Andrew, and once he had there was no doubt they loved each other unconditionally. It was Rory however, that was able to stop the tantrums before they started, at least some of the time.

Now at five years old, in the care of his loving parents for over three years, amazing progress was being made every day. The cereal box being knocked from the table was no longer accompanied by screaming and flailing limbs. It was just the box being thrown to the floor. Progress indeed.

As Rory rubbed Joseph's arm and shoulders, Andrew jumped up and opened the cupboard that held the boxes of cereal. "This one?" he asked. Joseph didn't react. "How about this one?" Andrew pulled another box from the shelf. Again, no reaction. As Andrew pulled the third box out, Joseph wiggled and then smiled. "Lucky Charms it is," he grinned and kissed Joseph on the cheek as he poured the cereal into his bowl. The two men looked at each other and smiled. Breakfast could now begin.

*****

"Joseph, I need you to get in the car so we can go to school. Tilly will bring you home in a taxi." Rory tried to keep his voice calm and even. The problem was they had this conversation *every* morning.

Taxis were Joseph's favorite form of transportation. He hated the subway, refusing to even go down the steps. Busses were absolutely out of the question. Their car was tolerable but taxis were preferred.

"Please?" Rory pleaded. "We have to get you to school. Mrs. Adams is waiting for you."

Joseph, visibly irritated they weren't going in a taxi, finally climbed into the back seat and into his booster seat. With a sigh, Rory strapped him in and checked Isabelle's seatbelt before climbing into the driver's seat and setting off for St. Luke's.

There were five kids in Joseph's class, all autistic. There was one teacher, Mrs. Adams, and two aides. The school would be hiring another aide especially for Joseph when he entered 1st grade in the fall. The donation that Andrew and Rory made each year would be going to pay their salary so Father James had even offered them a place on the interview panel, to which they readily agreed. Andrew was now on the school board. He had taken his mother's place when she'd finally resigned after thirty years, so it wasn't out of the ordinary for him to sit in on interviews.

As Rory pulled up in front of the school, he double parked and ran around to help Joseph from the car. One of the aides was waiting for him and Joseph went with her after giving his dad a big hug and a wet kiss on the lips. Rory grinned as he wiped his mouth and waved to Isabelle as she headed into the brick building. She didn't return the wave, obviously still upset at the hem of her skirt being lowered back to its original length. Rory chuckled to himself as he jumped back into the car and drove to his office.

He was incredibly fortunate to scale back his hours now that he was a father. He and Andrew treated their professional lives equally, neither job was more important than the other. It was imperative that they both were hands-on fathers. They decided from the very beginning that they would not leave the raising of any children they had to someone else. Andrew left for work first, leaving Rory to get the kids to school. Tilly, their nanny, picked up Joseph at school and brought him home, in a taxi. She worked with him on muscle control and music therapy, along with basic things like colors and numbers. Andrew left work first and picked up Isabelle on his way home. Then Rory met them in time for dinner and Tilly went home.

They had a housekeeper who made them dinner on the weekdays as neither Andrew nor Rory could cook. Their life before children consisted of eating out every night, but that was no longer an option. A nice home cooked meal as they all sat around the table was the preferred method and Agnes was an angel sent by God himself to their family. She took care of them like they were her own family.

This particular Thursday went just as any other day did. Andrew left for work. The kids were dropped off at school. Tilly left a message with his secretary when they arrived home safely just after one o'clock. Andrew left work at three and took a cab to St. Luke's and picked up Isabelle who was sitting on the brick wall as she always did. On the ride home they talked about what had happened at school, Isabelle chatting away like normal. It wasn't until they arrived home and were all sitting at the table having some cookies and milk that Agnes had made earlier in the afternoon, when it all changed.

The phone rang. It was Matt.

5.

David & Lindsey

Stepping off the plane at La Guardia International Airport with two very cranky children was not a great start to the day. Rachel, aged thirteen months, was desperately tired but refused to go to sleep. Lindsey had sung to her softly, given her the dreaded pacifier, tried massaging her, and even graciously accepted the lavender oil from a nearby passenger to rub on her hands...all to no avail. She was a stubborn little thing. Very much like her mother. Amanda, aged four, tucked safely in her daddy's arms, was also tired, but being more like her father, she just slumped in his arms and whined...a little.

After passing through immigration, they marched for miles to the baggage claim and waited, somewhat impatiently, for their luggage.

They'd spent the last ten days in Italy. Lindsey loved to experience the culture and food there, and David the art. They both wanted to expose their daughters to their passions and decided to include them in their vacation, even though Maureen had offered multiple times to have the girls stay with her. It was the first time they'd traveled with the girls and as the trip neared the end, Lindsey had questioned her decision several times, but now that they were back in New York, she was glad they'd gone as a family.

After her second daughter was born, David and

Lindsey had decided that they needed to reprioritize their life. Lindsey had scaled back at the restaurants, still holding the title of Executive Chef, but with more of an advisory, mentoring role. She spent a few hours at the restaurants each week, but worked on the new menu items in her own kitchen, making it possible for her children to be with her most of the time.

David had also changed careers. No longer the curator for the Atherton Gallery, he was their top-selling artist. Audrey Atherton had begged and pleaded and whined and pouted until he'd agreed to sell some more pieces. To date, David held the honor of being the artist whose painting had sold for the highest price in the gallery's history. He now stayed home full-time and painted when the desire hit him. Some days he sequestered himself in his studio and painted for hours. Other days the girls painted with him. And there were even days, and weeks, that he painted nothing, and loved every minute of it. Their home was filled with drawings and paintings of their girls. David and Lindsey's successful careers meant nothing when compared to their little family.

Growing up in foster homes, Lindsey took on the role of motherhood with a commitment that at times scared David. But with their second daughter now one year old and the talk of perhaps adding one more soon, as Lindsey's child-bearing years were coming to a close, she had relaxed a little and was the most loving mother David had ever seen. They were a happy family and delighted in their time together.

Finally loaded into a cab, they rode into the city and were relieved to get into their building and the girls and all the luggage into their apartment. With Amanda tucked into her bed, with her favorite stuffed animal in the crook of her arm, she was asleep in seconds. Rachel, on the other hand, wanted nothing to do with her bedroom. Even stepping through the doorway made her scream.

"How about a bath?" David smiled as he took his baby girl from Lindsey. "Shall we go play in the tub?"

Rachel tilted her head to one side and grinned. David kissed his wife and wandered off to the bathroom. Lindsey began dragging the suitcases through to the master bedroom in hopes that at some point during the day she could get them unpacked. She didn't have to be back in the restaurant until Monday so that gave her four days to get the laundry done and their lives back to normal.

"I need a vacation," she sighed as she heaved the girls' bag onto the bed. "I'm so tired."

Their plan had failed...miserably. She'd suggested that they fly home at night and that way the girls would sleep on the plane. It hadn't worked. It was 6:45 a.m. according the alarm clock next to the bed. Jet lag was going to be a bitch. Of that she was sure.

The giggling wafted through the apartment. She couldn't help but smile as she heard the sweet sounds of her husband and daughter laughing, singing and playing. Tiptoeing down the hall, Lindsey leaned in the doorway and watched David blow bubbles as Rachel giggled and lunged for the uncatchable little balls of air. Bare footed, David sat on the floor next to the tub and entertained Rachel until she finally yawned. He swooped her into a fluffy towel and kissed the bottoms of her feet. He smiled at Lindsey as he swung around. "Diaper?" he whispered, which sent Lindsey running to the bedroom. David lowered Rachel to his bed, Lindsey diapered and dressed her in pajamas and then, after shoving the bag onto the floor, they both laid down with Rachel between them. Taking one of her parents' hands in each of hers, Rachel closed her eyes as Lindsey hummed a lullaby and David rubbed her tummy. Within minutes, Rachel was asleep and David lifted her from the bed and carried her through to her crib.

"How long do we let them sleep?" he asked as he returned to his wife.

"Doesn't matter," Lindsey frowned. "We're screwed no matter what."

David chuckled. "Well, we can sleep or have a good time," he said as he wiggled his eyebrows.

"Sleep *is* a good time," Lindsey smiled.

David undid the buttons on his jeans and shoved them down his legs. Kicking them off, he pulled his shirt over his head and jumped on the bed and stretched out alongside his wife. "You sure you can resist this?" he grinned. Lindsey yawned. "You wound me!" he laughed. "But how about we take a nap?"

"Yes, please," Lindsey answered. "You can impress me later."

*****

"Holy shit!" David exclaimed, sending Amanda into fits of screams and immediately waking Lindsey from sleep.

"What?" Lindsey sat up, her eyes not able to focus properly. "What?"

Amanda ran around the bed to her mom and threw herself into her protective arms.

"Honey, it's okay. What's wrong? Shhh," Lindsey soothed.

"Dammit!" David muttered as he sat up, taking a couple of deep breaths. "I'm sorry Mandy girl," he offered. "You scared me, that's all."

Lindsey looked at David asking the unspoken question. Amanda was still crying into her mother's breast.

"I opened my eyes and she was right there!" David explained. "Inches from my face. Scared the crap out of me...for half a second," he added.

Lindsey bit her lips, trying not to smile, difficult because she found it quite amusing. "Amanda? Daddy's sorry for scaring you. Are you okay?" A muffled sob escaped from her daughter, but Amanda lifted her head and nodded. "Good girl," Lindsey smiled. She looked over at the clock. It was just past eleven. She closed her eyes and yawned and wondered if she could just go back to sleep...just for a few more minutes. Her eyes felt full of grit and her eyelids refused to stay open but then she heard Rachel yelling. "I guess naptime is over," she sighed. "Do you want to get into bed with Daddy?" she asked Amanda.

"I'm hungry and I'm thirsty."

"Let's get you something to eat then," Lindsey said, swinging her legs off the bed and stretching as her daughter skipped from the room.

"Sorry," David frowned. "She scared the shit out of me though."

Lindsey laughed and left to get the baby. Returning a few seconds later, she handed Rachel off to him and headed after her other daughter.

In the kitchen, Amanda had climbed up onto one of the stools at the counter and was impatiently waiting for her mother. "Milk, please," she commanded.

The refrigerator was not stocked. "No milk, honey. Juice?" Lindsey asked.

"I want milk!" Amanda wailed.

"How about…"

"Milk!"

Lindsey watched the meltdown rapidly approaching. Obviously, no one had had enough sleep yet. "Milkshake?"

Amanda's eyes opened wide. "Chocolate?" she asked.

Lindsey smiled. "Chocolate it is."

Ice cream, ice, chocolate syrup and some canned evaporated milk in the blender and milkshakes for breakfast averted the crisis. With Amanda now on the couch with a shake and watching cartoons, Lindsey returned to the bedroom. David and Rachel were sound asleep. Tiptoeing back out of the room, she made her shopping list and called it in to the market, hoping for delivery later in the afternoon.

Refilling Amanda's cup, Lindsey nestled into the corner of the sofa, Amanda snuggling into her side. Maybe the day could be salvaged after all.

*****

With the whole family awake and happy, David entertained the girls by dancing to The Wiggles in the living room while Lindsey unpacked suitcases and sorting everything into piles. The laundry got shoved in the wicker basket in the bathroom, the clean clothes were quickly put away in dressers and closets, and souvenirs were put in the spare room until Lindsey could decide what to do with them later. The gifts for her foster mother and David's parents she left on the bed. They would probably go and see Trudy on Saturday, and they would see Peter and Maureen on Sunday.

With the bag of art supplies in her hand, Lindsey opened the door to David's studio and stepped inside. The huge canvas stood directly in front of her. David had started it before they'd left on vacation, and although it was not finished, Lindsey already loved it. Staring back at her were two sets of beautiful blue eyes, with auburn ringlets tumbling over small shoulders. He had the amazing talent of capturing such emotion and personality in his paintings. This particular piece was going to Peter. David still had to add the whimsical elements to it, and then the "sprites" would be ready for Grandpa. That's what he called his two little granddaughters – sprites. David had taken the idea and created this magical painting that she was sure Peter would treasure. She couldn't wait to see his face when he saw it for the first time. Both Peter and Maureen doted on all their grandchildren, but Peter had something a little extra for all his little granddaughters. He had six now and each one adored him, too.

Lindsey placed the bag on the desk and left the painting behind her as she closed the door and went to join in the silliness in the living room. Dance parties were a regular occurrence at this Lathem home. She had no idea David was such a good dancer when she'd married him. She loved to watch his moves and so did the girls. But she didn't get the chance because the buzzer sounded. Their groceries had arrived!

Lindsey waited by the door and let the delivery man in with all the bags and generously tipped him on his way out. As she put cartons of milk in the fridge, Amanda got a hold of the remote and turned up the volume on the television, prompting Lindsey to cover her ears. Rachel screamed with delight and jumped right into the coffee table, smacking her forehead and bounced off, falling to the ground screaming in pain. David leapt to his baby girl and scooped her up checking her for blood.

"No blood!" he yelled, as Lindsey scrambled for the remote. Amanda ran in the opposite direction, delighted with the game now in play.

"Amanda!" Lindsey yelled. "Give me the remote control!" Amanda just laughed louder and ran faster.

It was at that moment that the phone rang. With the television screeching, Amanda laughing almost uncontrollably, Rachel screaming and holding her head, it was a surprise Lindsey heard it. Running to the TV, she pushed the power button, eliminating one of the noises and ran to the phone. It was Janie.

"Hi, Janie! How are you?"

6.

Ben & Sophia

Ben awoke to the all-too familiar sounds coming from the master bathroom. Heaving, wrenching, and vomiting. The sounds broke his heart....just as it did every time he heard his wife being sick. Alas, he was used to it by now. In the four years they'd been married, Sophia had spent many months of it in the bathroom, worshipping the porcelain god. Having recently received the joyous news that they would be adding baby number three to their growing family, they were both resigned to the fact that the next few months would be a challenge.

Alex was now sixteen and growing into a fine young man. Ben loved him beyond words and they had bonded immediately over baseball. But that bond, once a small strand, was now a thick and indestructible rope of love, trust, loyalty and respect. While Alex saw his biological father regularly, it was Ben whom he considered his father. It was Ben in whom he confided.

Alex loved his two younger siblings, too. Charles, or Charlie as he was called, had just turned four, and Lisa was now two...a terrible two, according to her mother. With the family expecting another baby in just five months, Alex had told Ben many times that he couldn't be happier with their growing family. Neither could Ben.

Walking through to the bathroom, the sight of his beautiful wife grabbing her hair, and her head all but in the bowl of the white toilet, Ben felt helpless. He crouched down next to Sophia and held her hair back as she finished throwing up. With his other hand, he reached for a washcloth and managed to twist the faucet on, soaking the cloth in cold water.

"Here, babe," he whispered, as she took it from him and wiped her forehead and mouth.

Ben fell backwards into a sitting position and spread his legs wide, pulling Sophia back into his arms. "I wish there was something I could do," he sighed as he kissed her hair.

"Me, too," she chuckled. "It would make it so much easier if I carried the babies but you had the morning sickness."

"I would," he said seriously.

"I know," she smiled and twisted around to face him. "I love you."

"Love you, too. Go back to bed and I'll make sure Alex gets off before I go to work."

Sophia nodded, grateful to be going back to bed. Ben helped her from the grey marble floor and tucked her into bed before going back into the bathroom to have a shower.

*****

"How's Mom?" Alex asked when Ben padded barefoot into the kitchen.

"In bed. I'm wondering if maybe your grandparents would watch the kids for a couple of hours this morning."

"That bad, huh?"

Ben frowned and nodded.

"You know, if you didn't keep knocking her up she wouldn't be sick," Alex teased with a chuckle.

"Ha ha," Ben replied. He poured himself a glass of orange juice and slid onto the stool next to his stepson. He'd always been sure he would never get married and certainly never have a family. Yet here he was…married with three children and one more on the way. And according to Sophia, they weren't done. She wanted a dozen children with him. She'd said it hundreds of times. She was even prepared to be sick for nine months to get each baby here.

Ben wasn't sure about a *dozen* kids, but he loved the three they had with all his heart, and was already falling in love with baby number four. Sophia would grab his hand and place it over her belly every time she felt it move. It was still too small for him to feel it yet, though. As he chugged his juice, he recalled watching Charlie's foot press against the confines of the womb and Ben would push back, only to have his son kick back at him. When he turned three, they enrolled him in soccer.

Lisa was a little princess. She was the most beautiful girl Ben had ever seen. She looked just like the pictures of Sophia as a baby. But when she'd turned two, it was as if a switch had been flicked and she turned into a beautiful little monster. Ben was counting down 'til her third birthday. Maybe the switch would flick back and his sweet little Lisa would return.

"Do you want me to call Grandma?" Alex asked,

interrupting Ben's thought.

"No, it's okay. Thanks. Do you need money?"

Alex shook his head. "I'm good. I have jazz band practice after school and I have money for a cab to get home."

"Home for dinner though, right?"

Alex grinned. "Yep." He finished his bowl of cereal and took the bowl to the sink. "Gotta go. Ray will be here any second."

"Have a good day," Ben smiled as Alex grabbed his backpack and left the apartment.

Miraculously, Lisa was still asleep. Charlie was in his room playing with Legos. "Whatcha making?" Ben asked when he went to check on him.

"A boat."

"Can I make one, too?"

"Okay," Charlie nodded.

Ben sank to the floor and leaned against Charlie's bed and began pulling pieces from the bucket while Charlie chattered away about his boat and the car he'd already built. While Lisa was a perfect miniature Sophia, Charlie was all Ben, right down to the little cowlick in his hair. Ben was absent-mindedly connecting blocks while gazing at his happy little boy. He pulled his phone from his pocket and dialed his in-laws. Fortunately, now mostly retired, they were happy to come over and watch the children so

Sophia could rest. They doted on their grandchildren and were very grateful that they lived across the street. Aldo and Gloria were welcome in their home anytime, day or night, and while Sundays were spent with the Lathem side of the family, many weekdays were spent with the Mannings. Ben was indebted to them for the care they took of Sophia and his family while he was working.

Each morning when Ben headed off to work, he understood why his brother had retired. Matt had worked extremely hard to build his company to what it was, and Ben had continued that work when he'd taken over. But as he left his family each day, he longed to be with them. He counted down the hours 'til he could return to them. And today was no different. He kissed Sophia tenderly on the cheek, told her that her parents had just arrived to watch Charlie and Lisa, and left the apartment, already missing them.

*****

By ten o'clock, Sophia had managed to crawl out of bed and stagger through to the living room. Sipping on some ginger tea and some dry toast, her spirits were lifted by the antics of Lisa, dressed in her princess skirt and tiara.

"Sing!" she commanded to her mother as Sleeping Beauty sang to the animals on the television.

"I know you, I walked with you once upon a dream..." Sophia began. "I know you, the gleam in your eyes is so familiar a gleam."

"You sing so pretty, mommy," Lisa said as she leaned on the seat cushion of the sofa where Sophia lay and fiddled with her hair.

"Thank you," smiled Sophia. "So do you."

"But if I know you, I know what you do," Lisa sang with heart. "You wuv me at once, the way you did once upon a dweam."

Sophia couldn't help but smile with joy as Lisa danced around the room waving her wand she gripped tightly in her chubby little hands.

"I see the next American Idol," Gloria chuckled as she came into the room. Sophia scooted her feet up and Gloria sat at the end of the sofa. "How are you feeling?" she asked her daughter.

"Better," Sophia smiled. "This helps," she said and nodded at Lisa still dancing and singing.

"She is adorable," Gloria agreed.

"What's Charlie up to?"

"He and your father are still playing with Legos. I think he's having more fun than Charlie," she chuckled. "Can I get you anything?"

Sophia shook her head.

"You need to try and eat something," Gloria said as she looked at the half-eaten piece of toast on the coffee table. "You're all skin and bone. That baby needs some fat!"

"Whatever I eat just comes back up. I go back to the doctor on Monday. I'll talk to him about it again."

The phone rang and saved Sophia from the same old

conversation with her mom.

"It's Ben," Gloria smiled and handed her the phone.

Sophia stood up and wandered down the hall to her bedroom. Once inside, she shut the door behind her and fell into the armchair by the window. They talked for a few minutes. He wanted to know how she was doing and if her parents were still there, to which she answered "fine" and "yes". Gloria and Aldo had no plans for the day and were more than happy to spend the hours with their grandchildren. Ben was relieved to hear that perhaps she would get some rest. He told her he loved her, which she repeated back and then they said their goodbyes.

As Sophia clicked off the phone, she let her head fall back against the plush fabric. *Maybe they won't mind if I just close my eyes for a minute,* she thought, and drifted off to sleep.

*****

Ben always tried to call home periodically throughout the day. He'd turned into his brothers...doting husbands and fathers, and he didn't mind...not one bit. He called to hear his wife's voice. He called to calm his heart. Sadly, however, the call was short today as he had a day chocked full of meetings. He still had three more before the day would be over and he could return home.

Emily buzzed to let him know his next appointment was waiting. As the door opened, he looked up from his desk to see his good friend Maria enter his office. He hadn't seen her in several weeks but as she walked towards his desk a smile lit up his face.

"You look fantastic!" he gushed as he stood and rushed around the desk to give her a warm embrace.

"No, I don't," she muttered. "I look like a whale."

"Nonsense! Pregnant women are beautiful. Can I get you anything? Water? Coffee?"

Maria shook her head. "The last thing I need is something to drink. I already go to the bathroom every twenty minutes," she huffed.

Ben chuckled. He completely understood. Well, he mostly understood.

Maria had married Alan Welton, one of the attorneys that represented MEL Holdings, a couple of years ago. Ben felt quite smug when he thought about their marriage. After all, he was the one who'd played matchmaker. And fortunately, once Ben was married, Sophia was more than happy to socialize with Maria now that she had her own man. Now, here sat Maria, happily married and expecting a baby any day.

"I thought Evan was coming?" Ben asked.

"He's sick with the flu so he asked me to represent the department. Is that okay?"

"Absolutely. Let's get the business over with then, shall we?"

*****

With lunch eaten and the kitchen cleaned, Gloria put Lisa down for her nap. She'd been at a full run all morning, so Sophia was sure she would sleep for at least a couple of hours. Charlie sat happily on the recliner and watched a classic Disney cartoon. Ben was adamant that his children grow up knowing about Donald Duck and his nephews, Mickey and Minnie and the rest of the gang. The music of Fantasia filled the room as Charlie clung to his blanket and was engrossed in the explosions of color on the screen.

"Really," Sophia insisted. "You can go home and rest," she chuckled. "You've earned it."

"Are you sure?" her mother asked again.

"I'm sure. Thank you so much for staying as long as you did. I love you both."

Aldo kissed his daughter on the cheek and he took Gloria by the hand and led her home. Sophia was feeling better. Her stomach had finally settled after a glass of ginger ale and with Lisa asleep all was quiet. It gave her a couple of hours to work on homework.

Taking college classes over the internet had been a brilliant idea. It had been Ben's idea and he *was* brilliant so it all made sense. She figured she had two more semesters and she would have completed her degree, something that she hadn't even imagined would actually come to fruition. Having a husband and a family made it difficult to get her studying done, but they'd worked it out. Ben was completely supportive of her decision to finish her education, and even though he'd reminded her over and over again that she would never have to worry about money, she needed to graduate...for herself. A few of the classes had required her to actually go to campus, but this semester, her two classes were both online, which was just as well given her propensity to worshipping the porcelain god. She could study when the children were asleep and that worked well.

Eighteen more credits was all she needed to graduate. Alex had decided to attend NYU and she wanted to be finished by the time he began. That only gave her one more year, as Alex was almost a senior in high school. How the years had flown by.

As Sophia worked away on her laptop, writing a twenty page paper, the words flowed and references that she had noted to use seemed to weave themselves together seamlessly. In some ways, she felt she had an advantage in her major of early childhood education, as she already had three children. But she was learning so much and feeling proud of her accomplishments so far. She was averaging an A- GPA and not feeling like she was neglecting her family.

After two hours of typing away, only getting up three times when her bladder refused to be silent, she had made an excellent start to her paper and hoped to have it finished by Sunday evening. The phone rang and she grabbed it quickly, not wanting the shrill sound to wake Lisa. She was enjoying the peace.

"Hey!" she smiled into the phone. "I thought you had a crazy afternoon."

"Sophia," Ben said. "Matt just called. Something terrible has happened."

7.

Paul & Nic

The days of taking a long hot shower were over. So were the days of sleeping in, a midnight run for pizza, and lazy Sunday mornings making love 'til noon.

Nic quickly rinsed the conditioner from her hair and shut off the water. With a towel wrapped around her she peeked out of the bathroom to see who was awake. Paul sat up in bed, leaning on the headboard, with both children crawling over him. Quietly, she shut the bathroom door and quickly dried off and stepped through to the closet and dressed in navy blue trousers and a button-up short-sleeved pale blue cotton blouse. Not having nearly enough time to do anything else, she quickly braided her wet hair and applied a small amount of make-up. Her kindergartners really didn't care what she looked like. Bending over to grab a pair of shoes, the button from her pants popped off and rolled under the shelf.

"Damn!" she muttered as she sat down on the bench and sighed. *Nothing fits anymore*, she thought as she glanced at her clothes hanging in front of her. Her eyes looked upward to the clear plastic tote on the top shelf. "Guess it comes down today."

Standing on the bench she just vacated, she stretched up until her fingers finally managed to touch the plastic.

"What the heck are you doing?" Paul bellowed as he

walked in, Annie clinging to his leg and sitting on his foot as he walked.

"Trying to reach my maternity clothes."

"You should have yelled. Come on. Move," he chuckled as he grabbed his wife around the waist and pulled her off the bench. "Annie? Can you let go for two seconds, please?"

"No," the three year old replied.

Nic rolled her eyes and pried her daughter from Paul, just long enough for him to grab the tote, lower it to the ground, and kiss Nic on the forehead. Then Annie threw herself at her father and grabbed his cheeks in her little chubby hands and kissed him smack on the lips.

"Thank you," he chuckled. "Now let's let mommy get dressed, k? Gregory?" he yelled. "Come on! Breakfast time." He left Nic in peace to rummage through the tote for something to wear.

In the kitchen, Paul sat Annie on a stool at the counter and opened the fridge and pulled out milk and eggs.

"Can I have Captain Crunch?" Gregory asked as he wandered in.

"Sure," Paul nodded. "Annie? Do you want cereal, too?"

She shook her head. "Eggs and toast."

He got to work feeding his kids, Gregory first, as he left for school with Nic. Now in first grade, he didn't like the fact that he had to wait in the kindergarten room with his mother until school started. That room was for babies and he was *not* a baby anymore. But he did like the perks of having his mother being a teacher at his school. He liked walking to and from school with her. It was time that he didn't have to share her with his little sister. And, sometimes he would have lunch in her classroom with his cousins who also went to his school. He liked to do that.

As Paul plated some scrambled eggs and a piece of toast for Annie, Nic rushed in and poured herself some orange juice. She chugged it down in just a couple of gulps and then grabbed her forehead when the pain hit.

"ARGH!"

Paul laughed. "You do this *all* the time. Brain freezes are avoidable, you know."

"Thank you," she smirked, as she rubbed her head.

"You have plenty of time," he added. "Have some eggs."

"Ew, no," she frowned. "The thought is not appealing this morning."

Though she didn't have morning sickness, there were some foods Nic just couldn't eat during her pregnancy. Eggs were near the top of the list. Watermelon, however, was not on the list and as she opened the fridge to return the juice to its shelf, she grabbed a large container full of it for lunch.

"I don't understand how a fruit that's basically water can sustain you throughout the day," Paul said.

"I could eat buckets of it," she replied. "But I'll take some pita chips and hummus too, k?"

He grinned and nodded. "Do I have ten minutes for a shower before you leave?"

"Yep," she smiled.

"Thanks," he said as he hurried from the kitchen.

*****

Now married for eight years, Paul and Nic had settled into a comfortable and happy life. Still a kindergarten teacher, Nic loved her job, especially being able to have her sweet nieces and nephews in her class, and her own children at least in the same building.

Paul was now the Executive Director of a non-profit organization that worked with veterans. He repeatedly reminded himself how lucky he was to have found a second career after leaving the Navy Seals that he loved almost as much as being a Seal, albeit considerably less dangerous. It certainly wasn't the same as the rush of a mission, or as physically demanding as being active in the military, but he knew that what he was doing now also made a difference in the world. And he strongly believed that the veterans deserved to have the opportunities he was working so hard to ensure they received.

Another wonderful thing about his job, was that his office time was flexible. There were many things that he could do from home and so two days a week, he stayed at home with Annie. It required discipline to actually work and not just play with his baby girl all day, but he was managing quite nicely, and it meant Annie was only in daycare three days a week. Not that daycare was a problem. There was a wonderful young lady in their building who watched her. Talk about convenient and she was thrilled at the prospect of watching the new baby if and when Nic decided to go back to work after her maternity leave was up, although no decisions had been made yet, as that was still a few months away.

It had been a wonderful surprise to announce at a Sunday family dinner that they were expecting another baby, only to have Ben and Sophia reveal that they, too, were pregnant. The cousins were due just ten days apart. Maureen couldn't have been happier. For so long she'd wondered if her sons would ever get married, let alone give her grandchildren and now here they were popping out babies every couple of years.

Paul was shaving when Nic walked up behind him and wrapped her arms around his waist. Resting her cheek on the damp skin of his back she sighed.

"You okay?" he asked.

"Mmm. I think we should go away this summer. Just the two of us. We can leave the kids with someone and have a few days all to ourselves."

"That sounds fantastic. Do you think you can leave them for long? Last time we left for a weekend, we came home on Saturday," he chuckled. "You made it all of one night."

"I know, but Annie's older now. She'd probably enjoy a vacation from us, too."

"Let's get through the next month and then we can

make plans."

"K," she agreed and kissed his skin before pushing away. "It's time for us to leave."

"I'll be dressed in a minute."

*****

Gregory was very much like his mother. He was going to be an intellectual. Paul could already tell by the way he did his homework; the fact he loved the science channel over cartoons; he would prefer to play with Legos over playing at the park. Annie, on the other hand, was probably going to follow in her father's footsteps and become a Navy Seal, according to Nic. In her short three years of life, she'd seen the inside of the Emergency Room five times. If it wasn't for the fact that Adam was their pediatrician, Nic would be worried that Child Protective Services would be paying them a visit.

Annie launched herself off furniture with reckless abandon. She purposely shoved Paul's keys into an electric outlet just to see what would happen. Wanting to fly, she climbed up the steps at her grandparents' house and launched herself into the air, escaping serious injury by landing on her Uncle Mark. He didn't escape injury and broke his wrist.

Privately, Paul was elated by his daughter's fearlessness. She would never let anybody push her around, either. At the ripe old age of three and a half, she possessed a kick-ass attitude and take-no-prisoners approach to life. But Nic worried about her constantly, so Paul tried his best to allow Annie her adventures, but in a contained way.

Like this morning, after spending thirty minutes on a conference call with the VA, he walked into her bedroom and found that his sweet daughter had built a tower of some kind with her bedroom furniture. She'd managed to lift her chair onto the table and had balanced her doll house on top of the chair. Now she was climbing up, already on the chair preparing to hoist herself onto the house.

"What on earth are you doing?" Paul exclaimed as he rushed to grab her before she toppled to the floor.

"Trying to touch the ceiling," she replied, as if it was the most normal thing in the world for her to be doing.

"Why?"

"Because I haven't yet."

Holding her against his chest, he stifled the laugh trying to get out. Then, without warning, he tossed his daughter high in the air and caught her as she came back down.

"Again!" she screamed as she giggled wildly. Her daddy obliged.

Over and over he threw her into the air and she became giddy with delight as she hit the ceiling with her hand each time she flew through the air. After a couple of minutes, Paul held her tightly and kissed her cheeks.

"There," he grinned. "Ceiling has been touched. Let's go and have some lunch."

*****

"I appreciate your help and look forward to seeing you," said Paul into the phone. "I know that you have been an amazing ambassador for our organization and I can't thank you enough."

Paul had been introduced to Fred Borsten by his brother, David. Several years ago, shortly after Paul had joined the organization that he now ran, Fred had been in dire straits. Through David's association with Lou, Fred's daughter, Paul had been able to assist Fred secure adequate housing and continued medical attention for his diabetes. Now Fred was speaking at events to help elicit donations, and also to encourage those veterans needing help, to come forward and ask, sometimes difficult because of pride.

Paul ended his conversation and typed up some notes on his laptop. After proofreading the document, he emailed it off to his assistant at the office. Stretching his arms high above his head, he stood and was just about to check on Annie, who'd been asleep for well over an hour when the phone rang.

"Hello?" he said cheerfully.

"Hey, Paul," came Mark's voice.

"Hi. How are you?"

"Not good. Paul? Something has happened…" Mark choked out.

8.

Tim & Beth

Beth had barely slept, spending most of the night tossing and turning. At one point, she'd crept from the bedroom, closing the door behind her so as to not wake her husband, and sat in the living room in the dark. Silent tears had soaked her cheeks as she'd muffled her sobs into a pillow.

When the shrill alarm sounded, she'd slapped it off quickly and slid from the bed. Standing in the bathroom door, she gazed at Tim sleeping peacefully. She'd let him sleep for a few more minutes before the ugliness of the day began.

Unable to put a coherent thought together, Beth stumbled around the bathroom, turning on the shower, brushing her teeth, throwing her pajamas on the floor in a pile. For the last few weeks, she'd known this day would come. She just hadn't wanted to think about it and by *not* thinking about it, she'd hoped that it would just be postponed indefinitely. No such luck.

Stepping under the scalding beads of water, Beth hung her head and let the warmth cascade over her. Tim slipping in behind her didn't even make her jump like it usually did.

"Morning, beautiful," he whispered as he nibbled on her shoulder while wrapping his arms tightly around her waist and pulling her back to him. She remained silent as he continued trailing kisses along her shoulders and on her neck.

"I...I don't think I can," she whimpered.

"I know," he replied with a sad smile. "But let me hold you," he said as he turned her around and pulled her against his chest. "I wish there was something I could say to make it all better...something I could do."

"Me too."

But there was nothing anyone could do. Not even the Veterinarian could help. Today was the day. Today she had to say goodbye and she had no idea how she was going to do it.

*****

While still working as an editor, Beth had not worked much over the past few months. Personal issues had kept her from being able to concentrate on the ramblings of others. However, she'd started a journal and found it occupied much of her time and Tim was encouraging her to turn it into a book. He'd said that many people would want to read it. Beth knew there might be a few who'd want to read her most personal thoughts, but she wasn't sure that she wanted to let them inside her mind...and her heart. Infertility was common, but also extremely personal and heartbreaking. Was she willing to expose herself like that?

Their struggle had begun a few years ago when they'd stopped all forms of birth control, deciding that they'd let nature take its course. After a year, Beth had gone to see her Gynecologist and discussed it with her. A few tests were run, on her and Tim, and she was diagnosed with PCS, Polycystic Ovarian Syndrome. Armed with prescriptions for drugs designed to help her conceive, they tried for over two years with no success. Holistic approaches were taken and were not realized. Having just undergone their third in vitro fertilization attempt a few days ago, they waited. Tim remained hopeful while Beth, plagued with hormonal fluctuations, waited for the doctors to tell her, once again, that it had not taken.

All that had happened over the past few years was documented in a Word document on her laptop. Everything. Not just the clinical procedures, but the emotional toll it had taken on her and her husband. And to make matters worse, her sisters-in-law were popping out babies left and right. Not that she wasn't thrilled for them all. She was. Always the first to volunteer to babysit, Beth found herself surrounded by nieces and nephews and thrilled with the opportunity. It was when she was no longer with them that her heart broke once again.

Tim was the eternal optimist. After each time they made love, or after each procedure, he would hold her in his arms and whisper, "This is it! Do you think we just made our baby?" And then he'd kiss her tears away when her period would come…the answer being a resounding "*no.*" It was all just way too hard.

The journal had been helpful. She'd been able to pour out her innermost thoughts and feelings and there wasn't anybody to judge her for them. She'd been honest and raw as she pounded away on the keyboard, leaving nothing unspoken…or un-typed. She hadn't even let Tim read it, although he knew what was in it. She was open with him and shared her feelings truthfully. They were a team and she didn't want to hide things from him, especially as her hormone levels fluctuated like a roller coaster. She needed him to love her unconditionally and she hadn't been let down by him once. Eventually she'd probably let him read it, just not yet. It was still too soon.

As Beth left the bedroom, she walked down the hall of their spacious apartment, a gift from Matt when she'd married Tim. Three empty bedrooms sat waiting to be filled with little bodies…the babies she craved. Andrew and Rory had discussed with them the possibility of adoption, but she wasn't ready to go there…yet. They had to exhaust all other avenues first, and then…well, they'd wait and see.

Continuing past the closed doors, she wandered through to the kitchen and poured herself a glass of milk. Walking through the living room, past the empty dog bed, she stepped onto the patio and closed her eyes. The city was coming alive as the sun rose over the tall buildings. It was going to be a glorious day. It was just too bad that her heart was breaking with each passing minute.

*****

Walking into the vet's office after lunch, Tim kept a firm grip of Beth's hand, squeezing every so often in a show of support and love. The receptionist smiled at them as they entered the waiting area and asked them to have a seat while she went and got the doctor. There were several other pet owners scattered around the room, each with their own best friend; a few cats, several dogs, a parakeet and a turtle.

Sitting on the vinyl covered bench for just a moment, the vet walked through the doorway and walked towards them.

"Hello Beth. Tim," he nodded. "Come on back."

They stood and followed him down the hall, past the exam rooms and into the back room, through the cat room and into the large area that housed the dogs that were ill or needing medical attention. There lay Cleo, Beth's faithful companion for the last nine years. With tears in her eyes, she hurried to the cage and knelt in front of her best friend.

"Hello, sweet girl," she whispered.

The doctor opened the cage and Beth pushed herself forward and placed her hand gently on Cleo's back.

"You are such a good girl," she cooed. "My beautiful girl."

Cleo didn't lift her head, but her eyes opened and she sighed. Tim's heart broke as he watched the exchange. He placed his arm on Beth's shoulder and wiped a tear that had escaped down his cheek.

"I will love you forever, Cleo," Beth continued talking to her dog. "You saved me so many times and I will never forget you." She continued to stroke her back and rub her ears. "You are forever my girl."

The cancer had spread quickly and silently. After two surgeries, the vet had said there was nothing more they could do. She was in constant pain and could no longer walk. The last three days had been spent at the vets getting a second, then third opinion. All were then same. The time had come. Beth had to say goodbye.

The I.V. was already in Cleo's front paw. All the vet

had to do was administer the liquid in the syringe and Cleo's pain would be over…she would be at peace…and Beth would be devastated…distraught and heartbroken. Cleo had been there for her, ever loyal, forever faithful. She had even brought Beth and Tim together. How would she survive without her girl?

With sobs pouring from her, Beth leaned in and kissed Cleo for the last time, and it was as if Cleo knew what was happening and she used her last ounce of energy to lift her head and lick Beth's hand, saying goodbye in her own way. Tim nodded to the doctor and he pushed the contents of the needle into the IV. In mere seconds, Cleo closed her eyes and exhaled her last breath.

*****

Sitting on the park bench half way between their apartment and Tim's fire house, Beth fondled the dog collar that she held in her hands. The leather was worn and soft…pliable from years of wear. Gut wrenching. Heart breaking. The tears wouldn't stop.

Tim held her close…his arm protectively around her as he sat beside her and silently comforted her as best he could. He shared her pain and her loss, after all, Cleo had been his dog for the past six years, too.

They'd sat for almost an hour watching other dogs play with their owners as they ran after balls and sticks and collected treats for behaving. Tim was just about to suggest they head home when his cell phone rang.

"Hey, Mark," he said into the phone. "Can I call you back?" But then his expression changed from concern to something more.

Beth turned her head and read his expression. "What is it?" she whispered.

"Oh, no," Tim choked. "No."

9.

The Obituary

After many phone calls and texts, it was decided that Mark would begin the necessary arrangements. Family members would be arriving from out of town starting tomorrow, but Matt didn't want to wait to begin the unpleasantness of planning a funeral. Mark agreed that it was better to get it over and done with so that the grieving process could begin. Never having dealt with a death as close as this, he sat on the sofa without even an inkling of where to begin.

"The first thing I did when mom died was to talk to the hospital," Katy offered, sitting down next to him and taking her husband's hand in her own. "Maybe we should go down there and see what they have to say. They'll have a whole department just for this sort of thing. They deal with it every day."

Mark nodded. "Yeah. That's the place to start."

Matt, on the other hand, flew into CEO mode, it being much easier than trying to deal with the emotional onslaught, immediately on the phone with the police, as he would be the go-to person in the on-going murder investigation. In fact, the two detectives handling the case were on their way to his apartment to get some background on "the deceased" as they put it. At first, Matt was put off by their callous nature, but Janie reminded him that they saw death all day long. It would be impossible to remain focused enough to do their job if they became emotionally involved with every one of their cases. Matt nodded and called Eddie, the doorman, to have him send up the detectives as soon as they arrived.

Andrew and Rory, along with Paul, had arrived at their family home within minutes of the phone call. Liko had stayed with Maureen after the police had left until her sons had arrived. They tried to talk to her but she had gone into "mom" mode and was trying to make snacks for everyone. It was going to be difficult to get her to sit down for more than two seconds. She was obviously in shock…and denial.

David and Tim went to the hospital. They needed to be with their father who was lying on a gurney in the hallway. The hospital was chaos, with some kind of bizarre chemical accident sending dozens of people into the E.R.

"Isn't there anywhere else you can put him?" Tim demanded of one of the nurses as she rushed past them.

"I'm sorry," she replied, genuinely apologetic. "But there isn't at this time. Please try and be patient."

"Tim, go home to Beth," David pleaded. "I'm fine here with Dad. And Mark and Katy just called to say they were on their way here. Beth needs you more than he does right now," he said nodding at his father lying still beside them. "There's nothing you can do here, anyway."

So Tim took his father's hand and kissed him on the forehead. There was no response. He hugged his brother and left.

*****

Matt sat at his desk, pen in hand. Some thoughts had come to his mind and he wanted to get them on paper before they were lost to him.

He put the needs of his children above his own. Dedicated to giving his children the best advantages possible. Kind hearted and giving. Responsible and honorable. Loved by all who knew him.

A tear dropped from his cheek onto the paper under his hand. *How could this have happened?* But Janie stepped into the room to tell him the detectives had arrived before he had the chance to try to come to terms with the tragedy.

"I guess this is where we hear the ugliness of it all," he frowned.

And ugliness it definitely was.

He appeared to be high on drugs when he demanded the cash from the till...in his early forties with nothing in his life but a long list of drug-related arrests and incarcerations. Janie thought it was sad. Matt was furious.

"So he killed a man over one hundred and forty-three dollars."

"It appears so," the detective replied.

I'd've given the piece of shit a million dollars to have him back again...to go back and do it all over and have it all be different now, Matt thought. But what was done was done and all of his money couldn't change it.

"Thank you for your time," one of the detectives was saying. "We're very sorry for your loss."

Janie saw them out and Matt grabbed his wallet and cell phone off the credenza and met her at the door.

"I'm going to the hospital," he said.

She nodded. "Okay. Do you want me to come with you?"

Matt shook his head. "Stay here with the kids. They're gonna figure out something's going on."

"Should we go to your mom's?"

Once again, Matt shook his head, knowing that his brothers were with her.

"Okay," she agreed. "Give him my love."

Matt kissed her cheek and pulled her into a tight embrace. This was where he felt safe. Here in his wife's arms was home.

"I love you," he whispered and then he left.

*****

"I should go to the hospital," Maureen said for the third or fourth time. "I should be with him."

Paul shook his head. "David says it chaos there. And besides, there's nothing that you can do. We'll stay here with you until we hear more from Matt. He just called to say he was headed over there."

With an audible sigh, she sat down and closed her

eyes. Her boys watched her carefully, making sure she didn't buckle under the stress.

"How about a cup of tea?" Rory suggested.

"Good idea," Maureen agreed, opening her eyes and preparing to stand.

"No! No, I'll get it," Rory insisted. "You stay there."

"I'm not an invalid!"

"Of course you're not. But let us do something for you for a change," Andrew said softly as he sat beside his mother. "Do you want to talk about it?"

"Talk about what?"

"About what's happened today," Andrew said. "It probably isn't good to keep it all bottled up inside."

"What's done is done," she replied. "Nothing I say will change that. I guess we should be grateful they weren't both killed, I suppose. But I think I should be at the hospital. I want to be there when he's discharged."

"David and Matt are taking care of that, Mom. Oh, here's your tea."

Rory placed a dainty cup and saucer on the coffee table in front of Maureen and then sat on the other side of her. "Can I get you anything else?"

Maureen smiled. "No, thank you. I just need to see Peter. I *need* to see him. Why can't I go?"

*****

Matt stomped through the Emergency Room looking for David. After asking three different nurses he was finally directed to a small dark room. David hugged him as he entered the room and for several seconds they just held each other, not saying anything.

As they separated, David spoke. "I'm so sorry, Matt."

Matt nodded and looked over at his father. His eyes were closed. He looked peaceful, with the exception of the cut on his forehead over his left eye. The paramedics had placed a small bandage over it but the blood had seeped through and left a small red stain on the bright white gauze, a stark contrast that made the events of earlier seem very real now.

"Apparently a murder and an assault are not high on the priority list," muttered Matt, as he stepped towards his father. "Have you even talked to a doctor?"

"Very briefly. He'll be fine. They've just given him a sedative because he was a bit overwrought."

"Naturally," Matt said.

"We can take him home as soon as he wakes up."

"Good."

"What's good?"

David and Matt swung around at the voice and rushed to the side of the gurney.

"Dad!" they both exclaimed, each one grabbing a hand.

"I'm fine," Peter muttered, trying to sit up.

"No," David said as he held him down. "Just lie there and relax. I'll go find a nurse."

"Matt," Peter said looking up at his son. "What happened? Where's Ray?"

*****

"I haven't told him anything," Matt whispered to Paul, as he opened the door to help his father from the taxi. "I want him to be with mom when he hears the news. She'll know how to comfort him."

Paul understood. As a Navy Seal, death was sadly a reality he had faced too many times to count, and having to share such horrible news should be done carefully. He leaned into the car and helped his dad slide out onto the sidewalk.

"What happened?" Peter demanded for the tenth time.

"Let's get you inside and then we'll tell you everything," Paul replied helping him down the steps to the family room door.

"Peter!" Maureen exclaimed and ran to the door to greet her husband. "Oh, God! You're hurt!"

"I'm fine," he grumbled. "Is Ray here?"

With a startled expression, Maureen looked to her sons. They guided Peter to his favorite armchair and settled him down with a pillow behind his back. Matt knelt in front of him and held one of his hands.

"Dad," he began. "What do you remember?"

Peter took a deep breath. "I walked into the market. I just wanted some aspirin for your mother. Oh, Maureen!" His attention immediately turned to his wife. "Are you alright? I never got the aspirin."

She smiled at him. "I'm fine, dear. Don't worry about me."

"And then?" Matt asked.

"There was a man…with a gun. He was yelling at the young man to give him all the money in the cash register. He was screaming and waving the gun around and I yelled at him to leave."

"Of course you did," Paul shook his head.

Peter had always stepped in when he felt someone was being mistreated. At work, at school, in the park, it didn't matter. He'd said that he felt a moral obligation to stand up for that which was right and he'd passed his sense of responsibility down to his sons. He'd always said that he had a duty to fight for those needing assistance. And a man with a gun pointed at him was *surely* in need of assistance. Even at eighty years old, Peter would never have backed away from that.

"And then?" Matt encouraged him to continue.

"He swung around and told me to shut up," Peter said. "And I told him that I would give him the money he needed if he'd just put the gun away, but he wouldn't. So I reached for my wallet and that's all I remember. I was going to give it to him so he'd leave but I guess he hit me." Peter reached for his forehead and winced as he touched the cut that was now causing his skin to turn bright purple.

"I should call Katy and have her come change the bandage," Maureen said.

"I'm fine," Peter repeated. "Tell me what happened, Matt."

"Ray ran in when he saw what was happening is the police's guess. The cashier said that he fought the guy for the gun, but…it went off, and…"

"And?" Peter asked, tears filling his eyes, somehow already knowing the answer to his question.

"And Ray was shot. He died before the ambulance got there."

"Oh, dear God," Peter cried.

*****

Raymond Charles Thomas, beloved father and friend, the obituary in the paper began, written by Matt and Ray's two daughters who had arrived in New York from Michigan on Friday afternoon. They were devastated and grateful to the Lathems for handling the funeral arrangements.

Separated from their dad in their childhood when their mother had moved them to her hometown of Detroit, the girls hadn't seen much of their father, but in recent years had opened up communication and were slowly becoming close with him again through email and phone calls. He was paying for their college tuition and spoke with them as frequently as possible. Their future with him had been mercilessly snatched from them and they mourned a man they were just starting to get to know. How cruel life could be.

Ray had been raised by a single mother in Harlem. His older brother had died at the age of seventeen in a gang related shooting and Mrs. Thomas had done all she could to ensure Ray didn't follow in his footsteps. And he hadn't. Joining the army, he'd served for eight years, spending five of them in the Middle East during Desert Storm as an Army Ranger. He'd been employed by a security firm for a couple of years before meeting Matt and accepting his offer of employment. He'd said many times that next to having his daughters, it was the smartest choice he'd ever made, working for MEL Holdings. He'd loved his job and had grown to love the family. When his mother had died a few years before, it was Matt and Janie who'd been there for him, whose shoulders he'd cried on, who had comforted him. They were his family.

Ray had separated himself from the life he'd had as a boy. He'd encouraged his cousins to follow in his footsteps, offering all the help they needed to get out of and away from the gangs that ruled their neighborhood and become respectable citizens, returning to school and being fathers to the children they'd sired. But many of them hadn't listened to him and they'd drifted apart, and once again Ray claimed the Lathems as his family.

And the Lathems claimed him. First a reliable employee and then a trusted driver, Ray became the man that Matt confided in and leaned on in times of trial. He was the loyal friend who watched over Matt's children, Ella and Christopher, like they were his own. And they loved him back. Matt didn't know how to break the devastating news to his kids. They were too young to experience such loss and be exposed to senseless violence like this. They would be robbed of their innocence but it couldn't be helped…he couldn't procrastinate too long.

The funeral service would be the following week. It would be a small affair. The girls wanted it to be private…they wanted to be able to mourn the loss of their father without hundreds of eyes on them. Ray wasn't a church-goer, and neither were his daughters, but they thought a religious service would be appropriate, so it was arranged with Father James that St. Luke's would hold the service. They also would respect his wishes and have his body cremated.

Leslie, the older of the two girls, had asked to speak with Matt privately over the weekend.

"Jackie and I have been talking, and, we know where Dad would want his ashes spread."

"Okay," said Matt. "Is there something that you need me to do?"

Leslie nodded. "We loved him, and we know he loved us, but, you should be the one to take care of it. I know he would have wanted it this way."

Matt nodded. "Anything you need."

"Will you take him to your house in the Bahamas and spread his ashes in the ocean? He loved it there. He spoke of the peace he felt there and how he thought he might like to retire there one day. It should be his final resting place."

"Of course," agreed Matt. "But why don't you do it? It would be…"

"No," Leslie interrupted. "He loved you like a brother. You were with him every day. Please?"

So it was agreed that Matt would take Ray to the place he loved most.

10.

Goodbye

It had taken almost four weeks, but it was decided that the entire family would travel to the Bahamas to say goodbye to their friend. The annual fundraiser was behind them, school had just let out for summer break and work projects were put on hold. Schedules were rearranged and the flight booked. It would be a bittersweet trip. Who didn't love a couple of weeks in a mansion on a tropical island? Yet, they weren't going for fun.

Peter and Maureen were the first to step onto the plane bound for Freeport. Each day Peter shook off a little more of the guilt he carried with him, but it was difficult for him knowing that Ray had given his own life in protecting him. Peter had thought of him as a surrogate son and his heart had broken just as it would if it'd been one of his seven boys.

Settled in their seats, the rest of the family piled onto the private jet. It was the first family trip they'd taken together since the Caribbean cruise several years before. *How things have changed since then*, thought Maureen, as she watched her children, their spouses, and all the grandchildren fill the cabin of the aircraft with laughter, chatter, and in some cases, wailing.

Joseph was very unhappy with the current seating arrangement and made his feelings known. He wanted desperately to sit near Alex, which meant Charlie had to be moved because he didn't want to sit by Isabelle. With great diplomacy and tact, Rory convinced Isabelle that she should sit with Annie, so her little cousin wouldn't be scared, and then Adam took Lisa with him and Shelby moved over by Amanda.

Chaos ensued for several minutes until all were seated, belted in, and ready for take-off. It was going to be a long flight.

*****

The house was ideally situated near Freeport on Grand Bahama. It sat just a couple of hundred feet from the water with a mile of private beach. It boasted over fourteen thousand feet of living space but with eight families, plus Adam, Tyler, Derek and Shelby, it felt slightly cramped.

The billiard room, den and music room were turned into bedrooms, with a few of the older grandchildren sleeping on air mattresses in the family room. Adam called dibs on the pool house and was happy with the private accommodations. Tyler wanted to share with him, but Adam adamantly refused. With everyone unpacking and grabbing snacks, Adam took the opportunity to grab some alone time, as he closed the French doors behind him after entering the pool house.

It was a large room with a small seating area and flat screen television on the wall, a dining table and four chairs, a small compact kitchen, a large bed full of decorative pillows, and a bathroom that contained a sink, toilet and large walk-in shower. The idea of being slightly separate from the rest of the family was appealing to him for many reasons.

He loved kids. He wanted children of his own. But he

was around them all day being a pediatrician and this break from work was needed. He'd recently lost two of his patients to leukemia and it had taken a toll on him. Some relaxation was what he needed, even though that was not was this trip was all about. He loved all of his cousins, but he also needed a break from them. The pool house was a perfect place for him to hide.

When the knock came on the door, he almost didn't answer, but then he saw her and jumped from the bed and opened the door.

"You're smart to claim this first," Shelby chuckled. "I wish I'd known it was here."

"Is this your first time here?"

She nodded. "It's magnificent. I can't imagine ever wanting to leave here and go home. The weather is perfect. The house is incredible, *and* the beach is just right there!"

"You know I didn't grow up with any of this type of stuff," Adam said, waving his arm around the luxury they stood in. "But it sure is a nice way to spend a couple of weeks."

"I know," nodded Shelby. "This a vast contrast to the house I lived in with my mother."

The statement sobered Adam. He didn't want to say anything to cause her pain as she remembered the unfortunate events of her childhood.

"I'm sorry," he stuttered. "I didn't mean to…"

"It's okay," she smiled. "I think after years and years of therapy I have come to terms with my past. I can talk about it. Well, *most* of it. It's almost like I'm talking about someone else…like all the terrible things that happened…that they *happened* to someone else…not me. I'm trying not to be that scared little girl anymore."

"Do you think about it?"

"Sometimes," she shrugged. "As crazy as it sounds, I think that maybe it all happened the way it was supposed to."

"How?" Adam was shocked. "Why would you think that?"

Shelby sat on the sofa and got comfortable. "My mom was a drug addict. Drugs were always more important than I was. Her boyfriends were usually men that supplied her the drugs. Basically, she sold herself to anyone who could enable her addiction. If it wasn't for…for what happened to me, I would never have been brought to the Emergency Room that day and I would have never met Katy. Then where would I be?"

"But rape is never…I mean, you shouldn't wish…you can't mean that…"

"No," Shelby answered his question. "No child should be assaulted as I was. That's still really hard for me to think about. And the nightmares are still all too real. But look where I am now? Look what I've done with my life? I thank God every day that I met Katy, and then Mark, and then…you."

"Me, too," he whispered.

The shrieks of laughter erupted outside as water from the pool splashed everywhere.

"POOL PARTY!" Mark screamed and cannon-balled into the deep end.

"Time to go swimming," Shelby grinned, and walked back to the house to get changed.

Adam watched her leave. No. He hated that her mother's boyfriend had raped her over and over again. He hated that she'd been beaten to a pulp. But he *was* glad he'd met her. He was very glad she was a part of his life.

*****

The last time Matt and Janie had been in their vacation home, just a few months before when they'd escaped the miserable winter weather in Manhattan, Ray had been with them. He'd sat on the beach with them and built sand castles. Ray had dug out buckets and buckets of sand and made a speed boat with a steering wheel and seats and he and the children had played for hours as they'd each taken a turn at *driving* the boat. Matt sat on the balcony outside the master bedroom and gazed at the sand...the very sand they'd all played in just last year. It seemed like yesterday and at the same time, it seemed like a lifetime ago.

It had been over four weeks since Ray had left them and it hadn't gotten any easier. Matt often found himself reaching for the phone to call him, or thinking he heard his voice in a crowd. He missed his friend. Terribly.

"Kids are all asleep," Janie smiled, as she stepped onto the balcony and sat next to her husband. "After the flight and playing all afternoon, they're wiped out."

"Me, too," he replied.

"Have you thought about how you want to do this?" she asked.

Matt closed his eyes and sighed. "I don't want to do it. I don't want him to be gone. I want him to walk through the door and say hello. I don't want to say goodbye. I'm not sure I can."

Janie stood and slid onto his lap, wrapping her arms around his neck and pulling him to her breast. If there was something she could do to take the pain away from him, she'd do it in a heartbeat. But she felt the same pain. Ray had been the big brother she'd never had. She loved him and missed him. Terribly.

Somehow they'd get through it. Together.

*****

"I think I'm old enough to have outgrown the kids' table," Alex scowled at his mother. Sophia nodded and he happily headed outside to eat his lunch with Ben.

Most of the women were in the kitchen arranging the kids and trying to get them to eat, which was always a difficulty when they were all together. It was much more fun to play with their food than eat it.

Beth stood off to the side, watching the mothers with their children. The last month had been the worst of her life. Now she stood in the lap of luxury in a magnificent estate in perfect weather. Yes, they'd come to say goodbye to Ray, and it was a somber occasion, but the family had decided to try and enjoy the trip. Ray wouldn't want them moping around. He'd want a blow-out party for his send-off. But that didn't make it any easier for her. She desperately missed Cleo and the anxiety over the last round of IVF was beginning to make her crazy. She'd waited until the day before they left on the trip to have the pregnancy test. The call would be coming any time now. Had it worked? Or would she, once again, be dismally disappointed.

"Aunt Beth? Are you gonna eat lunch?" Amanda asked. "You can sit by me."

"I would love to sit next to you," Beth smiled at her niece. She grabbed a bun and squirted ketchup and mustard on it and then added an almost charred hamburger patty and some cheese, lettuce and tomato and a handful of carrots and pulled up a chair in between Amanda and Isabelle.

Sophia threw her hand up to her mouth and ran down the hall to the bathroom.

"Poor girl," Maureen said, as she wiped up some sloshed milk from the counter, the newest sippy cup not holding up to the marketing claims on the packaging. "I hope it gets better for her soon."

The other women agreed and Beth bit into her hamburger. She'd be thrilled to have morning sickness morning, afternoon and night if it meant she could have a baby. She wouldn't complain one bit.

But for now, she would just enjoy her precious nieces and nephews and pray that one day she'd get her miracle. Hopefully sooner rather than later.

Tim watched his wife through the doorway and instinctively knew what she was thinking by the way she looked at Amanda seated beside her. He saw the longing looks…the sadness in her smile. She couldn't hide it from him. He wondered what he could do to cheer her up…to make her forget her heartache for just a moment. As his phone rang in his pocket, he didn't have time to consider the answer to his question.

He didn't recognize the number. "Hello?"

"Is this Tim Lathem?"

"Yes."

"Oh, good! This is Dr. Ringer. I've tried your wife's phone but she didn't answer."

"Hello, Dr. Ringer. Ah, she probably doesn't have it turned on right now. We're out of the country. Is there something you needed?"

"Well, I needed to give you an update. Is this a good time?"

"Sure it is. Is it good news? Should I get Beth? Or should you tell me and then I can find a way to break the bad news to her?"

Dr. Ringer laughed. "Would you like to break the good news to her?"

Tim gasped. "Good news?"

"Very good news," he replied.

That evening, after all the children had been put to bed, and all the adults had shared several well-deserved bottles of wine, one by one, each couple headed off to their rooms, Paul and Nic, and Beth and Tim remaining on the patio overlooking the beach.

The waves gently lapped on the sand and the moon cast a beautiful golden reflection across the water. There was a slight breeze that was warm on the skin and Beth asked for a glass of wine for the second time.

Her first request earlier in the evening, Tim had said he'd forgotten when he came back from the bar with a can of cola. She'd shrugged and drank half of the can. This time she was a little more insistent.

"Please remember my wine this time," she'd called after him, as he strolled inside.

"I think I'm gonna call it a night," Nic smiled. "I'm tired!"

"Okay," said Paul and helped his wife from her chair. "We'll see you guys in the morning."

"Night," Beth smiled, as they left her alone of the patio.

Tim returned a moment later carrying two glasses. He handed one to her.

"This is water," she frowned. "Do we need to get your hearing checked?"

"I'm not getting you any wine."

"Why not?" she said, irritation in her voice.

"Did Paul and Nic go to bed?"

"Yes," Beth scowled as she sipped the ice water.

"Beth? I have something I need to tell you."

"That sounds ominous," she replied. "Lay it on me," she sighed.

"You can't have any wine, or *any* alcohol, for the next little while."

"What?"

Tim grinned, unable to keep a blank expression on his face. "Dr. Ringer called today."

"What?"

"Dr. Ringer called. We're going to have a baby!"

*****

"What the hell?" Matt exclaimed as he sat up straight.

"Somebody screamed," Janie said jumping from the bed and grabbing her robe.

"Stay here!" Matt ordered as he ran from the room and down the stairs, Janie following close behind him.

At the foot of the stairs they met Mark and Katy who'd also heard the noise. They were then joined by Andrew and Rory.

Peter stood at the top of the stairs. "What was that?" he barked.

"I don't know," Matt said as he picked up one of the children's cricket bats that lay near the stairs.

"That's going to defend us all," Mark chuckled.

Matt ignored his brother and stalked through the darkened house towards the children in the family room. All was quiet and all the children were accounted for. As he turned, he saw a silhouette on the patio. He tiptoed in that direction. A squeal came again and then laughing. Matt drew back the bat and stepped outside through the open doors.

"Oh, it's you!" he sighed with relief as he saw Tim and Beth in each other's arms. "We heard a scream and…"

"Sorry," Beth grinned. "That was me."

"Are you alright?" Matt asked, concern immediately back again.

"We're fine!" Tim smiled. "All three of us."

*****

The next morning was bittersweet. It was the day that had been set aside for Ray's ashes to be washed away in the clear turquoise water. But the excitement and joy that filled the house was palpable. The news that after years of disappointment Beth was finally pregnant lifted the sadness that had encircled the Lathems for the past four weeks. As they said goodbye to Ray, they also rejoiced in the coming arrival of another precious baby.

At eleven o'clock, the family met together at the water's edge. Matt held a silver urn in his hands as he solemnly walked a few feet into the warm water and quietly said his goodbyes. Tears were shed, memories were remembered and the ashes washed away quickly into the ocean.

Several minutes went by before Matt could turn and face his family. His tear-stained cheeks spoke volumes. It was hard to say goodbye. But he had and it was time to let Ray go.

11.

The Wake

Several years before, Matt and Ray had attended a funeral for a member of the security team at MEL Holdings. He'd died in a motorcycle accident that had shocked the company and blanketed them in grief for several weeks. He'd been a well-liked and beloved member of the work family and the church had been overflowing with those people whose hearts he'd touched during his short thirty-two year life.

The two men had sat on the bench of the church grieving with everyone else when Ray had turned to Matt and quietly whispered, "This is depressing. I want my life to be celebrated when I die."

At the bar later that day, as the men he used to work with toasted him, Matt and Ray again had a conversation.

"I want there to be party when I go," Ray had said. "I want people to miss me, sure. But I also want them to be glad they'd known me and to celebrate it. I don't think I could stand it if it was a morose affair."

"My parents and my tailor will be the only ones to miss me!" Matt had joked.

"That's B S and you know it!" Ray had replied. "You'll find a woman that will make that heart of yours melt and then you'll find the fountain of youth and you won't ever get old and you'll live forever."

"Unlikely seeing as though I plan on never letting a woman have the opportunity to rip my heart out and stomp all over it with her five hundred dollar stilettos. I am a confirmed bachelor…mark my words."

Ray had laughed…a knowing laugh…like he didn't believe a word Matt had said. And obviously, he'd been right. Matt met Janie just a month later.

As Matt watched Ella and Christopher play in the pool, the long-ago conversation reverberated in his head. Ray didn't want people mourning him. He wanted his family and friends to celebrate his life.

Finding Mr. and Mrs. Urain, the caretakers who lived over the garage year-round and took care of the house and the family when they were in residence, Matt discussed with them his idea for a party the following evening; music and dancing and lots of great food, with decorations and entertainment. He asked them if they could arrange it on such short notice.

"For you Mr. Matt?" Mrs. Urain had said. "We can do *anything* for you and Miss Janie."

*****

With her brow wrinkled and her lips pursed, Shelby sat on a chaise under an umbrella on the beach. For the past school year, her fourth year of medical school, she'd been working as in intern at a hospital in Newark, New Jersey. Now that she'd taken her finals and had completed several months of round the clock Emergency Department bedlam, it was time to move on to the next phase of her career. Having had to wait two weeks after finals to see whether or not she'd passed all her classes had been painful enough, but now Shelby was anxious about where she would be accepted for her residency. Applying all over the eastern United States, she hoped a hospital close to New York would accept her. For the last four years the city had been home and she'd grown to love it and desperately wanted to stay. That, however, was no longer up to her.

"You look lost in thought," Adam said, as he sat down on the sand sharing her shade out of the midday sun.

"Just thinking about the future...where I'll be headed in a few weeks."

"You've applied to several really good facilities. I'm sure they'll all want you."

"Johns Hopkins already said no. So did Concord. But they weren't my top choices, so fingers still crossed."

"So Beth Israel and Mount Sinai are still on the table," he encouraged. "You can't beat either of them."

In the weeks and months following her brutal attack when she was fourteen years old, Shelby had survived by focusing on one day at a time. In the beginning, it was more like an hour at a time. But as the years passed, with the help of caring and exceptional doctors, her physical and emotional wounds healed and slowly but surely, she began to think about the future.

She'd attended support groups. In fact, on occasion, she still did. Meeting with other women who'd gone through unspeakable cruelty and abuse, humiliation and shame, had helped her to realize what she'd wanted to do with her life. With her personal experience and her commitment to helping others, psychiatry was her field of choice. Many teachers and faculty during her pre-med days in Boston, and medical school in New York, had suggested that over the course of her education she'd probably change her mind several times as to in which field of medicine she truly belonged. They'd been wrong. Her resolve had never wavered. She'd been determined. There were still several years of residency and then fellowships before her dream would be realized, but it would all be worth it.

Dr. Margot LaVaughn had been her doctor in Portland for several months before she'd moved to Wisconsin to live with her grandmother. There, she'd seen Dr. Michael Inglethorpe who had also been crucial to her recovery. In Boston, she continued to see a psychiatrist, Dr. Elsa Weaving, who'd encouraged her in her career path and had even written letters of reference for her when applying to medical schools. These three people had left a lasting impression on her and she felt it was almost a calling to continue in their footsteps.

It was so close she could taste it.

"Is there something else you're worried about?" Adam asked, seeing something else in her eyes.

Shelby shrugged with her left shoulder and sighed.

"Tell me," he insisted. "Maybe I can help."

She shook her head. "I'm fine. I just don't like waiting. I keep checking my email hoping that my fate has been revealed, but...nothing yet."

"It will come," he reassured her. "But in the meantime,

let's go swimming." He yanked his t-shirt over his head and stood, holding his hand out to her.

Shelby paused. Hesitantly, she swung her feet over the side of the chaise and accepted Adam's hand. With an unsteady hand she fidgeted with the cover-up that covered her swimsuit. Looking down at her hand, she shuddered ever-so-slightly, but Adam saw.

"It's okay," he whispered and took her hand and held it in both of his. With his thumb he caressed the soft skin and bent his knees so he could look at her in the eye. "We've all seen it before."

With a deep breath she nodded once and pulled the fabric over her head and tossed it on the chair. Her skin looked pale against the black of her bikini. Her hand immediately found the scar on her stomach, just a couple of inches below her belly button and to the left. It looked like a surgical scar to anyone who didn't know her history, but to Shelby it was the only physical reminder of her horrific past. The stab wound had healed but she often wondered if she would ever be able to look at it without the visions of the bastard who'd inflicted it on her.

"Shelby," Adam whispered, trying to keep his emotions in check and not let his voice crack. "Let's go swimming."

She looked into his baby blue eyes and managed a smile. Then she took his hand and pulled him down the sand to the warm Caribbean water.

*****

For twelve years Shelby had been part of the Lathem

family. Every member had accepted her as a sister, a daughter, a granddaughter, an aunt. And every member of the family loved her unconditionally.

The first four years after leaving Portland for Wisconsin, she visited Katy in New York on school holidays. With Adam being six years older than her, at first, they didn't spend much time together. But once she'd declared pre-med as her major and was in college, the age difference wasn't so noticeable and the two found themselves in deep conversation at family events and on vacation.

A few years ago, when the whole family had spent the week of the Fourth of July in the Hamptons, Adam had thought they might be becoming more than just friends. After a long walk on the moonlit beach one evening, she'd taken his hand as they'd strolled back to the house and when Adam had tried to kiss her, she'd bristled and dropped his hand quickly.

"I can't," she'd said. "I don't know if I'll ever be able to have a relationship. Or at least a normal one," she'd confessed.

So Adam had lightened the mood by telling her that his last girlfriend had told him he kissed like a dog when she'd broken up with him. They'd laughed and tried to decide what that actually meant and he hadn't attempted to get close again.

But that didn't mean he didn't want to. In fact, since she'd moved to New York, and was living only a short subway ride away, he'd become quite creative in coming up with excuses to see her. Being a doctor only helped his cause. He'd offered help with studying and would bring her takeout and Frappuccino's, all in the name of *understanding what she was going through*.

During her second year of medical school, she'd begun to open up to him about the attack and how she'd been trying to use the experience positively...how she could empathize with her future patients, understanding the uphill battles they faced in recovery. They'd talked for hours and hours about the weeks and months of abuse that led up to the violence that landed her in the ER and her attacker in prison. Adam knew it all and Shelby had admitted late one night that she'd assumed he'd disappear from her life now that he'd learned all of her dark secrets. It'd had the opposite effect. The admiration and love he felt for her had only been strengthened by her vulnerability and in the fact that she trusted him enough to share it all with him.

He was a successful young pediatrician and was ready to settle down and have a family of his own. He'd at one time thought it might be with Shelby but she still wasn't ready and had made her reservations about any kind of intimate relationship known repeatedly. So Adam had dated - had had a lot of *first* dates, a few second dates, and a scarce number of third dates. There wasn't anyone that he was as comfortable with as he was with Shelby...and she wasn't interested.

*****

Bob and Cynthia Urain had both been born and raised on the island. They loved their home and they loved their job. For most of the year, they lived, just the two of them, on the beautiful estate. They kept the house in immaculate condition and took care of the family when they were there relaxing.

The Urains loved the Lathem family. Matt was a kind employer who paid them generously and was kind and undemanding when he was in residence. *Everyone* loved Janie and the Urains were no exception. She asked about their grown children who now lived in Florida and after Cynthia's mother who was suffering from Alzheimer's. The Lathems paid for the facility that cared for her, even though Cynthia protested. Matt insisted, telling them that it was the least he could do for them after all they did for his family. And besides, what better thing to do with all his money than to help those people he cared about?

As much as the Urains loved the children, Ella and Christopher loved them back times ten. Christopher used to follow Bob around the house and the gardens as he inspected the gardener's work, or the contractors if they needed plumbing work or the roof fixed. He would try to imitate the faint accent that Bob had and would have the family in stitches over his attempts. Ella wasn't interested in cooking with her mother at home, but when they came to their vacation home, she placed her apron over her head and spent hours as Cynthia's sous chef and loving every minute of it. In fact, Cynthia was such a positive influence for Ella that with her and Maureen's combined efforts, in just a couple of days they'd managed to help Ella understand that *all* food was good…just in moderation. Matt was incredibly grateful.

So when Matt had asked for their help in having a celebration, they pulled out every stop and called in every favor they had to ensure a magical party was what he received.

The vans started arriving just after lunch. The first to be unloaded held tiki torches and thousands of twinkly lights that were soon strung all over the patio of the house. A bar was set up and liquor and soft drinks were delivered by the crate. The DJ arrived next with massive box speakers that were placed on each side of the pool, ready to fill the air with drum beats and mumbled lyrics. By five o'clock, the catering van pulled into the semi-circular driveway and servers in shorts and flip flops hauled tray after delectable tray into the kitchen, awaiting the appropriate hour to plate it all on the tables being set up next to the pool.

The children buzzed with excitement and Matt looked on with satisfaction as the final preparations were made for their celebration to honor Ray. As Tim and Beth sauntered through the great room, Matt turned to his right and watched the aura of joy they carried. This celebration would be for them, too. There was nothing more deserving of a party than the upcoming arrival of a much-wanted, already adored baby.

Beth had called her parents and informed them of the happy news. They were naturally thrilled with the addition to the family. Rupert, Beth's older brother, had married but had yet to produce a grandchild, so Beth's baby would be their first.

Beth had also decided, after capturing in her journal her thoughts and feelings after the blessed phone call from her doctor, that she would, at some point, turn her very personal writings into a book. Struggling with infertility was not a unique problem known only to her. Just the clinic she'd visited regularly had hundreds of couples dealing with the exact same thing and the knowledge that she'd finally been able to do the one thing her heart craved, conceiving a child, had given her the desire to share her experience with others. No matter how personal and how private it was, she wondered if there hadn't been a higher meaning...a purpose behind the experience.

Tim had been completely supportive when she'd broached the subject with him. He'd even suggested she keep a daily account of her pregnancy, too. She'd liked the idea.

Now they stood watching the bustling all around them, but stood entwined in each other's arms as unconsciously they each had a hand over her flat belly. Matt smiled at the sight. Remembering back to the day that Janie had announced the wonderful news that they would be welcoming a baby was one of the happiest days of his life. He understood the joy his brother was feeling and he couldn't have been happier for them.

"I think it's fantastic that we'll be having a party tonight," he said. "Ray would be happy to know that his wake will be combined with a celebration for your news."

"He was a good man," Beth smiled. "And he will be missed more than any of us realize, I think."

Matt nodded but felt in his heart that he already knew just how much he would miss his friend. He had missed him terribly each day of the past few weeks and didn't see how the pain was going to go away anytime soon. But today was not a day to mourn so he tried to push the grief from his mind as he watched his children run around the patio, the excitement obvious as they giggled and skipped with their cousins.

Ben had Lisa in his arms and chased after Charlie who was dashing for the pool. With a swoop he reached out and scooped him into his other arm about three feet from the edge. Handing Lisa off to Alex, they headed for the beach to join Paul who was already building sand castles with Gregory and Annie.

David was not far behind his brother, Amanda running beside him, singing a merry little tune, and Rachel on his shoulders, one chubby little leg on each side of his head. She was laughing and patting her daddy on the head, urging him on toward the sea.

Andrew and Rory had Joseph in between them and they were swinging him high in the air as they walked. If you listened closely, you could hear the faint laugh escape from his lips. Isabelle and Christopher noticed them leaving and quickly fell in beside them, not wanting to miss out on any of the fun.

Ella was wandering around with Cynthia, as she supervised the deliveries and set-up. Matt chuckled. If his daughter didn't choose event planning as her career, he'd be surprised.

The rest of the family was in the house, scattered. His parents were in their bedroom resting. Peter hadn't been the same since the shooting. It had taken an emotional and psychological toll on him that had left the family struggling with how to help. Maureen had repeatedly told them that time would be the healer. Hopefully the party would, too. Matt was counting on it.

He headed back through to the media room. A Yankees game was on the television. He fell into the middle of the sofa, between Derek and Tyler, and watched, somewhat interested, until Cynthia announced that everything was ready and the party could begin.

*****

All the beautiful little girls were in party dresses and all the boys in their best church outfits. The women rivaled the pages of the best fashion magazines and the men were dressed to kill. The Bahamas are known for the laid back and relaxing atmosphere. Shorts and flip flops were the uniform. But Ray deserved nothing but their best and their dress showed it.

With a warm breeze and the smells of deliciousness wafting through the air, the DJ began the speakers thumping with a lively song that had all the girls skipping and the women wanting their men to dance with them. The bartender poured drinks and champagne bottles popped with a delicious trail of bubbles pouring from the long necks. Stainless steel lids were removed from trays of mouth-watering delicacies and the grill was already producing burgers and hot dogs with perfect grill marks for the children. As the sun dipped lower and lower, the thousands of tiny white lights sparkled brighter and brighter.

One of the first things Janie had done to the house after they purchased it, was to have a wrought iron fence put up in the corner of the patio. She wanted her children to be able to run and play but be in no danger of falling into the pool. Now it was filled with children, laughing and playing, safe, allowing their parents to also enjoy the evening without worry.

On the outside, to strangers, the Lathem clan looked not only wealthy, but happy, too. And they were. Although tempers occasionally flared, and differences of opinions made for healthy debate, the brothers were all best friends and their spouses had also become inseparable. They were a close knit group and when choosing the company they'd best like to socialize with, they were happiest with each other. Laughter, good-natured teasing, joking and conversation filled the air as the adults ate and drank and celebrated.

Maureen sat next to her husband and joyously watched her family. In ten short years they had grown in leaps and bounds and she wasn't sure her heart could hold any more love. Yet they'd just learned that another baby was coming and the excitement she felt was overwhelming. As all the younger grandchildren sat at tables and ate a smile formed on her lips.

"You look beautiful, my love," Peter said as he reached for her hand and brought it to his lips for a chaste kiss.

Maureen smiled and sighed. "There are moments like this that couldn't be any more perfect."

"Except that we are celebrating the life of a man who is no longer with us."

"My darling," Maureen whispered, fully aware of the guilt he felt. "The only person to blame for Ray's death is that vile creature who shot him. This is not your fault and I know that Ray would *not* want you blaming yourself."

He exhaled and dropped his head. "How can I not feel guilty? It was because of me he was there!"

"Well, if you're going to play that game, it was my fault then! I was the one who needed the aspirin. You went there for me!"

"This is not your fault," Peter declared forcefully. "Not ever your fault." He looked horrified she would even suggest such a thing.

"That's right…it isn't. And it isn't yours either. It was a tragic thing that none of us predicted, but I tell you what. He would've gone into that store even if he'd known what the outcome was going to be. He was that kind of a man and we should be grateful we had him as part of our family for as long as we did. I know that I can never understand or comprehend what you went through that day and I pray to God that it never happens again, but by golly, Peter, we need to move on. For Ray."

"Amen!" injected Matt, who'd silently approached his parents and overheard their conversation.

Peter looked from his son to his wife of nearly sixty years and nodded. "For Ray," he whispered.

12.

Ghosts

Tummies full. Feet tired. Eyelids heavy. The party had been a smashing success. As little princes and princesses were carried to bed, and the vans loaded and driven away, the lights of the house dimmed.

There remained only four by the pool: Derek, Adam, Tyler, and Shelby. Derek and Tyler fell into conversation about a project in Atlantic City that MEL Holdings was in the middle of developing. That left Adam to announce he was going to walk down to the beach. Shelby offered to join him.

In silence, they flipped off their shoes, Adam rolled up his pants and they headed for the moonlit water. In all the world Adam was sure he hadn't visited a more peaceful stretch of sand than that which lay under his feet. The property stretched for half a mile on either side of the house and the privacy was welcomed and appreciated.

The water lapped at their feet, occasionally covering them up to their ankles. The water was warm and soothing as the sand gradually collapsed under their toes. It was almost a full moon and even though it was now close to midnight, the beach was light and magical.

"That was a wonderful way to pay tribute to Ray. I'm sure he approves," smiled Shelby.

"Approves?"

"Yes. I'm sure he does."

"You think he's aware of our party?" Adam was skeptical.

"Of course I do. He's somewhere with his brother and his mom having a party right along with us."

"So you believe in heaven?"

"I believe in something," she replied. "I don't want to think that when we die that's it. That would be a terrible way to live."

Adam didn't respond. He just kept walking, gazing off into the horizon.

"Don't you believe in God?" she asked, breaking the silence.

Shrugging his shoulders, Adam considered her question. "I don't know," he answered truthfully.

"What about when your dad died?"

"It was a nightmare…those months before he died. I prayed every single day that he'd get better and he didn't."

"I'm sorry," she said as she placed her hand on his arm.

Adam smiled and placed his hand over hers, holding it to his skin. "He just gradually got worse and worse until he died. If there is a God, he ignored me."

"You don't think that maybe God let him die so that he wasn't in pain anymore? So that your family could begin healing?"

"I guess I've never thought of it that way."

Shelby grinned. "The great and mighty Dr. Anderson doesn't know it all?" she teased lightly.

"Hardly," he chuckled. "The older I get the more I realize how little I really do know. I'm learning things from my patients and their families every day."

"Kids are amazing, aren't they? They teach us so much. I was playing with Amanda this evening and she was telling my why her daddy paints pictures. You know what she said?"

Adam shook his head.

"She told me that her daddy painted her mommy's face so that other people could see the happiness in her eyes and that would make them happy. That's coming from a four year old. I realize it isn't some unheard of revelation or anything, but to have that kind of wisdom…insight is…is…"

"Out of the mouths of babes," Adam nodded. "They just tell the truth. No pretenses, no hidden agendas, just life as they see it. It's refreshing."

"It is," Shelby agreed.

"Do you want kids?"

The change in Shelby was physical. She pulled her

hand from Adam's and folded her arms across her chest. Her pace quickened and her lips pursed. Without thinking, Adam grabbed her arm and swung her around to face him, stepping within inches of her face.

"It's just a question."

"It's a loaded question."

"Tell me."

Her eyes dropped and Adam lifted her chin with his hand and held her gaze.

"I'd love children," she whispered. "But I can't see myself having any."

"Why?"

She stepped out of his hold and Adam let her go. They began walking back the way they'd come.

"I'm not sure I'd be a good mother and I don't want to fail. If you kill a plant, well…it's not the same as ruining another human being."

"You'd make an excellent mother."

"How do you know that? It's not like I had a good example or anything." There was bitterness in her voice. She rarely spoke of her mother, the pain still there, lurking, always present.

"There are lots of people who have complete asses for parents and who become the most loving and kind parents themselves. Look at Lindsey. Nic. Rory. Our own family has multiple examples of defying and defeating the circle of abuse and abandonment. You are kind and smart and have love to give. Don't sell yourself short. And don't deprive a child of your heart. Don't deprive yourself."

Slowly, they made their way back to the house. The patio was now empty. Derek and Tyler must have gone to bed.

"Do you want a drink?" Adam asked, as they walked to the French doors.

Shelby shook her head. "No. I'll see you tomorrow," and she headed inside, closing the door behind her.

Adam watched her silhouette walk through the great room and disappear. *She will make a wonderful mother...and the perfect wife.*

*****

With each year that passed, Matt's love for his wife grew. Their legs still entwined, the beads of sweat on their bodies glistened in the moonlight that was streaming through the open doors to their private balcony. Making love to Janie was his favorite way to spend his time and the last thirty minutes had been extremely pleasurable.

Fingers laced together and bodies in harmonious rhythm, they'd built to a peak so high, they'd fought to catch their breath as they plunged, crashing and exploding in orgasm that left them limp and satiated and Janie quickly falling into a deep and restful sleep.

Matt lay awake, his fingers mindlessly tracing patterns on the warm silky thigh that lay across him. His wife's breathing was hypnotic and relaxing as his eyes focused on nothing but saw everything. His entire family was here, under his roof. The experiences of the past few weeks had driven home the fragility of his peace and the shortness of life. One day, in the not too distant future, he would lose his parents. Death would claim them and leave him to step into their shoes. He was able to shoulder the responsibility. He just didn't want to. He didn't want to think about it but the thought lay siege upon him every so often and it was difficult to rid himself of the impending loss.

As his eyelids closed, he saw his friend…smiling…happy. He heard him laugh and his eyes flew open, only to confirm he lay in the dark, his wife next to him.

He'd heard Ray laugh as sure as he knew his own name. And then, in his mind, he heard as much as he felt the words, "I'm okay. Be happy."

A faint smile crossed Matt's lips as a tear escaped and fell quickly to the pillow. "Goodbye, my friend," he whispered, and pulled his wife into his arms and closed his eyes, drifting off to sleep.

*****

Shelby silently opened the bathroom door and crept down the hall to the music room that was her bedroom for the visit. It was a small room, but faced the beach. Bob had set up a roll away bed for her and it was comfortable enough. There was an oversized stuffed chair that sat next to the window with a matching ottoman that called her name. Snuggling into its' softness, hugging her knees, she looked out at the water and the moon light dancing across the ripples.

She'd been mad at Adam for asking her about wanting children. It was a thought she'd pushed from her mind. What right did she have to bring children into this world? She feared she would be as miserable a mother as her own. It was best not to think about it. *Besides,* she shrugged, *I'd have to have sex to have a baby.* She unconsciously shuddered.

Shelby had not had a boyfriend. She hadn't been on a date. Well, not a real date. She'd gone out with friends, met someone for coffee, or for a drink to blow off some of the pressure of medical school. She'd sat in the park for lunch or gone to a movie with a man, but it had never been a date, just two friends doing the same thing at the same time...together. The idea of getting close to a man scared her senseless. Dr. Weaving had encouraged her to spend time with men in safe situations...public places like crowded restaurants and theaters. She'd also told her that in time, a physical relationship would not seem quite so repugnant to her, but that day had still not arrived. The idea of some man putting their hands on her made her physically ill. Over the past few years she'd let men try to kiss her and each time it'd ended in the same way. She'd pushed them away and had ended up trembling and nauseated. There were only a handful of men that could touch her...in a non-sexual way, Adam being one of them. But's that because she knew there was nothing other than a sisterly affection he held for her. And that was safe...nonthreatening.

Adam had been her best friend since she'd moved to New York. He'd helped her study, brought her food during finals and let her whine and complain about the stresses of medical school, all while trying to finish his own residency and start his own career.

No. Adam didn't scare her. Adam was safe.

The breeze blew through the window, making the lightweight curtains dance and twirl. Slowly, her eyelids became heavy and fluttered closed, allowing her to drift off to sleep.

But it wasn't a calm sleep. Her dreams were memories, stirred up from the past, of her mother and things she wished she could forget once and for all. Left alone in a dark room, she was hungry and cold and when the door opened she looked up with anticipation, only to see *him*. Panic rose through her entire body and she violently shook as he took a step closer and then another. Pushed into the corner of the room, there was nowhere else to go. She was trapped with no way out.

From somewhere, the words of Dr. LaVaughn came to her child mind. "He can't hurt you anymore." Shelby spoke the words to *him*. She'd said it and he heard her. His head tilted and his brow furrowed. She stood on wobbly legs and said it again, a little bit louder. He opened his mouth to speak, but didn't. So she said it again much louder. "You can't hurt me anymore."

Her eyes flew open and she inhaled sharply. She still hugged her knees as the curtains whooshed with the gentle breeze. The moonlight still danced on the water and all was quiet in the house.

"He can't hurt me anymore."

13.

Awakening

For half of her life, Shelby had been seeing psychiatrists, the first being court-appointed in Oregon. Yet a dream had been one of the most powerful forms of therapy she'd had. A dream where a little girl had had the courage to say what her adult self had been unable to articulate. And it was life changing.

Stretching in the white sheets, Shelby smiled. The sunlight poured through the window, just as the moonlight had a few hours before. The air was crisp and her mind was clear. It almost felt as though she was on the precipice of a new beginning…that a new chapter was starting and the pages were all blank just waiting for her to write her own story.

What a wonderful way to start the day, she thought as she stood and stretched again. The possibilities were endless.

As she quickly dressed and made her way downstairs, activity had already begun. Cynthia was cracking dozens of eggs into a huge bowl and little feet were running everywhere. Walking to the huge island in the kitchen, she pulled out a stool and slid next to Sophia who was sipping on some orange juice. Pleasantries were exchanged and Janie offered her a cup of coffee, which she accepted graciously. Taking a sip, she noticed Adam shuffle through the glass door and fall into an arm chair just beyond the kitchen in the great room.

"Morning, sweetheart," Janie called. "Coffee?"

Adam grumbled his reply sending Janie to the task of filling another cup and then refilling the coffee maker, ready for the rest of the family who hadn't yet descended.

"You didn't sleep well," she frowned as she handed the cup to her son. "Go back to bed."

Adam thanked her for the drink as she hurried back to help Cynthia with the task of making breakfast. He sipped from his cup slowly.

He hadn't slept well. Tossing and turning most of the night, he finally got up before dawn and went for a run. Since his days of playing baseball in college, he'd used physical exercise as a way of keeping his mind clear and focused. This time, however, it hadn't worked.

The thought of Shelby becoming his wife had shaken him. He'd never thought of her as a potential partner. She'd been a friend...a *good* friend but she had rebuffed his single attempt at moving past that and he'd respected her wishes and backed off, even though he thoroughly enjoyed her company and used every possible excuse and reason to see her as often as he could.

But wife? No. That thought hadn't entered the realm of possibility. He didn't even know that was what he'd wanted...until last night when it had bulldozed him.

Shelby was the perfect package. Her blonde hair and blue eyes made her look like the girl next door, but her full lips and perfectly rounded breasts made her a candidate for Playboy magazine. She was voluptuous, no doubt about it. And now that the thought of her as his wife, an intimate partner, was in his head, and he couldn't shake himself free of its grip.

He watched her over the rim of his cup. She was bright and happy as she chatted with Sophia and Janie in the kitchen. The image that came to his mind made him choke on his coffee as he tried to stifle a laugh. When he and Tyler were young, they would watch Baywatch with their dad. Barely clad women would run along the beach, everything bouncing in perfect synchronization. As Shelby flicked her long blonde hair over her shoulder, in seemingly slow motion, that Baywatch image popped into his head and had him wiping the spilled coffee from his chin and his shirt.

Shelby swung around to see him muttering as he wiped the small puddle from the sofa.

"Just as well it's leather," he mumbled to himself.

"You okay?" Shelby asked as she came to stand right in front of him.

Adam looked at her long longs, up over her denim shorts and button up shirt that hung open, exposing her breasts clad in a hot pink bikini top. Her long blonde hair fell over her shoulders and her blue eyes danced with merriment.

"Fine."

"Need a towel?"

"No."

"You get up on the wrong side of the bed?"

Adam frowned. It wasn't her fault he'd fallen hopelessly in love with her without realizing it. "Sorry." He attempted to smile. "I didn't sleep very well."

Shelby smiled and reached for his cup. "I'll top that off for you," she said and headed for the kitchen.

I'm so screwed!

*****

White puffy clouds hung in the sky and warm turquoise water lapped the sand. It was another perfect day. Matt and Bob were setting up a volleyball net on the beach, with lots of help.

"I wanna do it!" demanded Annie as she pried the stake from Matt's hands.

"NO!" Amanda wailed. "Me!"

Matt was no longer amused with his nieces. They had turned a ten minute operation into twenty-five and they still weren't done. "Paul? David? You wanna come get your daughters so I can finish here?"

Paul jumped up from the fort he was building with Gregory and ran in Annie's direction. David, on the other hand, was fighting a battle with Rachel who kept trying to toddle into the water.

"I'll get her," Adam smiled, as he leapt from his chair and ran to rescue Matt.

Without additional help, Matt and Bob finished the set-up quickly and Matt headed back to the house to find the volleyball. Adam sat with Amanda on his lap and sang nursery rhymes.

"The incey wincey spider climbed up the water spout," they sang, Adam even doing all the actions. "Down came the rain and washed the spider out."

Amanda giggled at his exaggerated hand movements and Adam laughed and tickled her until she fell off his lap onto the soft sand.

"My turn!" yelled Charlie, who'd been playing in the sand with Gregory. He jumped onto Adam and clapped his hands. "Bob the builder CAN WE FIX IT?" he shouted.

"Bob the builder YES WE CAN!" Adam continued.

Joseph hurried over to the chair and stood next to Adam as he sang. Annie ran over and stood next to him and then joined in.

"Bob and the gang have so much fun, working together they get the job done," Adam sang out with gusto. "Okay, all together now," he yelled, with squeals coming from the kids.

"Bob the builder CAN WE FIX IT? Bob the builder YES WE CAN!" They all sang out.

"Yay!" Adam clapped. "You guys are great singers." And one by one they left to go back to what they'd been doing, playing in the sand.

"I didn't know *you* were such a great singer," Shelby chuckled as she climbed into the chaise next to him. "How do you know all the lyrics?"

"I'm a pediatrician," he laughed. "I *have* to know my stuff. It's part of the job requirement."

"So do you watch Nickelodeon on the weekends," she grinned.

"Yes," he nodded. "It's how I relax and unwind."

Shelby laughed.

"Actually, we have a TV in the waiting room and Bob the Builder is a favorite among the crowd I hang with," he smiled. "I have been known to dream about Bob and Scoop, you know."

"Oooh, how very erotic," she winked.

"Ha ha," he smirked.

"I think it's great, actually," she smiled. "You must be a very good doctor."

"I'd like to think so. Ella and Christopher haven't complained *too* much about me."

"Are you talking about me?" Christopher yelled from a few yards away.

"Yes," Adam yelled back. "About how you cried like a baby when you had your shots."

"I did not cry at all!" Christopher rebuked. "Not one tear."

"Just kidding ya, bud," Adam chuckled. "You were

very stoic."

"I was," he nodded with a serious expression. "What's stoic?"

Adam and Shelby laughed and Christopher turned his attention back to the action figures he was burying up to their necks.

Shelby leaned back on the chair and closed her eyes, a smile on her lips. Adam watched her from the corner of his eye. He watched her breasts move up and then down with each breath she took. As she relaxed, her lips parted slightly and Adam couldn't tear his gaze away. For several minutes he focused on her…on her lips…her breasts…her hands placed innocently over her stomach. The thoughts that ran through his head were as far from Bob the Builder as a man could get.

Yep! I'm royally screwed, he thought.

*****

Shelby had opened her eyes with a start. Not knowing where she was, she sat up and looked around. *On the beach…I remember.* Adam was no longer beside her. He was running on the sand trying to hit the volleyball. Diving with one arm extended, he missed. Cheers erupted on the other side of the net.

"Match point!" yelled Mark. "Come on you pansies. Put up a fight," he tormented his opponents.

Adam stood, brushing the sand from his chest and stomped back to his brother. They were playing two on two. Adam and Tyler against Mark and Paul. It wasn't even close.

Paul served and Tyler got his hand under the ball, shooting it into the air. Adam timed his jump perfectly and smacked it over the net…right into Paul's hands. The ball came down at Adam's feet.

"Oh, yeah," Paul chest bumped his brother. "Unstoppable!"

Shelby watched with amusement. The family was tight but when it came to friendly competition, it wasn't *friendly* at all. Adam and Tyler looked dejected. They were younger and faster than Paul and Mark, but had still lost…badly. Being the good sports that they were, the four men fist bumped each other and headed for the bucket of ice that held cold beers Beth had just delivered from the house. The men collapsed in the shade with a bottle and rested briefly before Paul rescued Nic from a very tired three year old.

Adam emptied his bottle and then stood and turned to Shelby. "Wanna go for a walk?"

"Sure," she replied. Lowering her sunglasses to the bridge of her nose, she stood and followed Adam down to the hard wet sand then fell in alongside.

They walked for a while in companionable silence. Adam kicked at the water lapping at his toes and stared off out at the sea.

"It's so beautiful here. Almost makes you want to not go back, huh?" she sighed.

"Sadly, I'd run out of money very quickly," Adam

chuckled. "And really. How long can you live in paradise before you get bored?"

"Bored?" Shelby was shocked. "I feel like I haven't had eight hours of continuous sleep in years. It feels so good to crawl into bed and stay there without the alarm going off, or my cell phone or pager. I think I could crawl into bed and stay there for a few days."

"And then?" Adam grinned. "Once you'd caught up on your sleep you'd get bored."

Shelby shrugged, but grinned. Adam waded into the water past his knees. "Wanna swim?"

She shrugged off the shirt she wore and unbuttoned her shorts, once again hesitation as she exposed her scar to the world. Adam noted the slight pause but ignored it and waded further into the calm water. He stood and waited for her to join him as the water lapped gently at his waist. He heard her behind him and as he turned a wall of water crashed across his face. Shelby erupted in laughter as Adam wiped the water from his eyes. "You're mine," he growled.

"ARGH!" she shrieked as he dove for her. Flinging herself to the side, she swam as quickly as her arms could paddle but he was too agile and dove underneath her.

Grabbing her waist Adam tugged and pulled her backwards as she squealed with laughter and under the water she went. As they both came up for air, they found themselves with barely any space between them and when Shelby lifted her arms to wipe the hair clinging to her cheek, her breasts grazed across his chest.

He gasped. She noticed…and froze.

"I can help you," he offered in almost a whisper, and cautiously…carefully…gently pushed the strand of hair from her face. He leaned in and placed a sweet kiss where her hair had been. As he pulled back, Shelby closed her eyes and licked her lips.

For such an innocent and unconscious act, it sent lightning bolts through Adam's body, his awareness of her body so close creating tension where tension shouldn't be. Falling backwards, he put some distance between them and laughed. "I *always* win a water fight."

*****

On the balcony of the house sat Janie and Katy, each nursing a Piña Colada and relaxing.

"Did you see that?" Katy shot up from her chair.

"I did," Janie replied.

"Well, it's about flippin' time!" Katy turned to Janie and smiled.

"Do you think there's something going on?"

"I don't know but I sure hope so."

The two women watched as Adam fell backwards into the water and swam back to the shore. He and Shelby were laughing and obviously enjoying each other's company.

"I've wanted her to meet someone who would be kind

and understanding," Katy said. "I never thought she would see what was right in front of her the whole time."

"Well, we don't know what this is...yet," replied Janie.

"No," Katy agreed. "But it doesn't mean that we can't help define it."

"Remember how much you liked Maureen *helping* you and Mark," Janie chuckled.

"Oh, that was different."

"How?" Janie asked.

"Well, we were already together...already madly in love with each other and we both knew we were committed to the relationship. This," she pointed down to Adam and Shelby on the beach, "is obviously still in the exploratory stages. And besides, we aren't anything like Maureen!"

"Oh, yes?" Janie grinned.

Katy snorted and ignored her friend. "You can tell by their body language. They haven't slept together. They're very awkward around each other."

"You seem to be able to tell an awful lot by one little kiss," Janie chuckled.

"I know Shelby. She'd going to need some prodding...some encouragement."

"And we are the ones to do that?"

"Definitely!" Katy grinned.

14.

Prodding

"What on earth are you doing?"

Katy looked behind her to see Mark standing with his hands on his hips waiting for an answer.

"What does it look like?" she growled.

"Pouring gallons of milk down the sink, that's what. What the hell are you doing that for?"

"We *need* to be out of milk."

"Why," Mark asked, but he wasn't at all sure he wanted to know the answer.

"So we can send Adam to get some more."

"Of course!" Mark nodded, mocking his wife. "That makes perfect sense. Yes. Cynthia stocks the house with groceries so that you can waste perfectly good milk, all for the obvious reason of sending Adam to get more. How silly of me to ask."

Katy rolled her eyes and summoned him closer with a flick of her head. "We need to give Adam and Shelby an opportunity to be alone," she whispered.

"Because?"

"To let things progress naturally."

"It's not natural if you're forcing them together."

"Semantics," she hissed.

Mark chuckled. "And what *natural* things do you think will come of them being alone together?"

"*That* we have to wait to see."

"And this all makes perfect sense to you?"

"Of course it does," she snapped back. "Sometimes a little prodding is all that's needed to encourage people to see what's right in front of them."

"I clearly remember a certain someone who did not enjoy being prodded," he smirked.

"Oh, don't you start, too," she warned. "This is *not* the same thing."

"If you say so."

"I say so," she replied sternly.

Mark chuckled, kissed her on the cheek and then wandered out of the kitchen just as Janie came down the stairs. "Are you in on this?" he asked her.

"In on what?" she replied innocently.

"Okay," Mark laughed. "I'll be outside if you decide you need to get rid of all the cheese, too."

As Janie entered the kitchen, she saw four milk jugs standing on the granite counter.

"Done!" smiled Katy.

"No one saw you?" Janie asked looking worried.

"Just Mark."

"So now we wait," Janie nodded.

*****

Shelby had offered to take Lisa down to the pool so that Sophia could rest. She blew up the inflatable ring and sat Lisa in it and walked down the steps into the water. Lisa shrieked with joy as they paddled around and splashed, Shelby enjoying herself just as much as the two year old.

Adam watched through the glass doors of the pool house. He sat at the small dining table and closed his eyes as he listened to them giggle.

There has to be a way to help her understand what a wonderful mother she'd be, he thought. The idea that because such vile things had happened to her meant she wouldn't be a great mom baffled him. He knew that to be completely false and wanted Shelby to realize it. But how?

He didn't have a chance to dwell on it though. Janie knocked on the door, forcing his eyes open. He yelled for her to come in and she walked in to find her son doing nothing, just as she'd hoped.

"I need you to run into town for me. Could you

please?"

Adam shrugged. "I guess. You're not sending Cynthia or Bob?"

"Cynthia has already started dinner preparations and Bob is helping Peter with something," she lied. *Well, it isn't a total lie,* she told herself. Cynthia was peeling potatoes, but she had no idea where Bob was or what he was doing, but he had to be doing *something*.

"Alright. What is it you need?"

"Milk."

"How? We had like five gallons in the fridge this morning!"

Janie shrugged. She wasn't a good liar. Better to keep it simple. "It's all gone." That *was* the truth after all.

"Fine. Just write down exactly what you want," he said as he stood and walked over to his flip flops.

Janie turned and all but ran back to the house, almost knocking over Matt as she flung open the French doors looking for Katy.

"Okay, he'll go, but he's going now," she blurted to Katy who was coming down the stairs.

"Now?"

Janie nodded.

"But Shelby's in the pool!"

"I know!" Janie replied.

"What are you two going on about?" Matt asked.

Taking two steps at a time, Katy flew down the stairs and out to the patio. Ripping off her shorts and t-shirt, she dove into the pool and swam to Shelby and all but yanked Lisa from her hands.

"My turn," she exclaimed, leaving Shelby with a confused look on her face.

Shelby stood up, the water at her waist and watched Katy bob down the pool with Lisa in tow. She walked to the steps and climbed up and out just as Adam exited the pool house.

"Here you go," Janie smiled at him as she handed him a list on a post it note, the keys to the car, and a wad of cash.

"I have money," he frowned.

"Just take it," she smiled, pushing it into his hands.

Shelby brushed past them as she walked to the bench that held her towel.

"Why don't you take Shelby?" Janie suggested.

"Um, okay," Adam stuttered.

"Shelby?" Janie swung around. "I need Adam to go

buy milk. Why don't you go with him?"

"I'm wet."

"You'll dry off in the car. It's a warm day," Janie said.

Matt, watching the conversation, shook his head in disbelief. Katy flicked water at him and when he looked down at her she shook her head and hissed, "Shhhhhhh." He chuckled and walked into the house.

"Yeah, okay," Shelby shrugged. "Let me grab my sandals."

Within just a few minutes the two had walked to the garage, climbed into the Jeep and were pulling out of the driveway. Janie collapsed on the chair by the pool and buried her face in her hands.

"What?" Katy asked her.

"That was horrible!" she muttered. "I don't think I can do that again."

"Good!" came the voice from the doorway.

Janie jerked her head up to see Matt looking down at her. "You two should stay out of this."

"Why?" Katy said. "There are obviously sparks there. We just need to provide some oxygen to fan the tiny little flames."

"Good grief." Matt rolled his eyes.

*****

The drive to the market was about fifteen minutes. The picturesque scenery was worth the trip. Miles of white sand lay outside of Shelby's window with the bluest of blue water for as far as the eye could see.

"I can't imagine why Leslie and Jackie didn't want to come," Shelby frowned. "It's so beautiful and peaceful here."

"I've only met them a couple of times," Adam said. "They weren't very close to Ray, well, not until recently. From what Matt said, the divorce was anything but amicable and once his ex moved to Detroit, I think she hoped Ray would be out of their lives permanently. And it's sad," he added. "Ray was one of the kindest men I've known. To deprive your children of their father out of spite is awful. I think it must have taken an enormous amount of strength to show such love for their father and ask Matt to scatter his ashes."

"How?"

"It would be hard to accept that your dad's boss was more of a family to him that you were. Who did Ray spend holidays with? Us. Who did he vacation with? Us. And Jackie and Leslie knew it."

"I guess," Shelby said, although unconvinced.

Adam noticed her skepticism. "They asked the person who knew Ray the best, spent the most time with him, to say goodbye. I think it's a very unselfish thing for them to do."

"But Matt asked them to come and they refused."

"Would you want to have gone with a family you barely knew?"

"Probably not."

"It's made me think about what I would want my family to do after I die."

"Huh? Why?"

"Mom and Matt have their funeral already planned. They've bought plots here on the island. Wills are all signed and everything is taken care of – they have left all questions answered. I'd like to do the same."

"I don't see what the big deal is," Shelby shrugged. "You'll be dead. You won't know…or care."

"But the family I leave behind will. I want it to be as painless as possible."

"Then I guess it's a good thing I won't be leaving any family behind when I die," Shelby snorted.

"That is the saddest thing I've ever heard!" Adam replied.

"Why?"

"If you die without a family to mourn you, it will have meant you've *lived* without a family."

"So?"

"So?" he repeated. "It means you've been alone…your entire life."

"So?" she said again.

"Don't you want somebody to laugh with? To spend the evenings with? To make love with?"

"That just opens you up to pain. I've seen pain and I'm not interested in inviting it back to live with me permanently."

They drove the rest of the way in silence.

*****

That night as Adam lay in bed, Shelby's words rolled around and around in his head. How sad it was to know that to her, family meant pain. The idea was so foreign to him that he couldn't even begin to understand it.

Unable to sleep, he threw back the sheet and climbed from the bed. Stepping into the clothes he's just taken off, he headed outside. Looking up at the main house, most lights were off, so he wandered around through the garden and headed for the beach.

A silhouette stood before him as he stepped onto the sand. It was either Matt or one of his uncles…all the brothers looked pretty much the same from behind and in the dark. As he moved closer, the figure swung around to see who was approaching.

"Adam," smiled Matt. "Can't sleep?"

"Nah. You?"

He shook his head then turned back to the peace of the sea. "It's calming to just breathe the air and listen to the water."

"Can I ask you something?"

"Sure," Matt nodded.

"Before you met Mom, you weren't going to get married again."

Matt nodded again.

"So what made you change your mind?" Adam asked.

Matt chuckled. "Your Mom did."

"How?"

"You want the long version or the short version?"

Adam shrugged.

"Let's sit," Matt said as he walked to the beach chairs. Once settled, he took a deep breath and began. "How much do you know?"

"Well, you met on the plane when Mom went to New York for her vacation. You spent some time together and then she came home. You missed her and went to Portland a few weeks later and told her you loved her and were married in August."

"That is the *very* abridged version," Matt chuckled. "But accurate enough."

"So there's more to the story." It was more of a statement than a question.

"Oh, yeah. A whole lot more. You know I'd been divorced...twice. Both complete disasters and neither of them involving any kind of love or emotion. But then along came your Mom and...well, she knocked the air from my lungs. And the few days I spent with her in New York were the happiest of my life, up until that point, of course," he grinned. "She was nothing like the women I knew and when she left to go back to Portland, well, let's just say that I was left an empty shell. Once I decided to go and beg for her to let me be a part of her life, I knew what I wanted and it was the whole thing; the woman, the commitment, the trust...everything! And only with her. If she'd said no, well, I don't want to think about it."

"She didn't say no."

"No, thank God," Matt smiled. "She didn't. And now I have four amazing kids and a life I'd never even allowed myself to dream of."

Adam listened, pondering Matt's words. "Shelby doesn't want a family. Not a husband or kids...nothing. She says it will cause too much pain."

"I'm not surprised," Matt whispered.

"Really?"

Matt shook his head. "Adam, do you understand what her family was like? Can you imagine being a child and having to deal with a mother who's a drug addict and letting her boyfriends do whatever they wanted to you? The horror that she must have faced, well, I can't even imagine. I grew up with parents who adored me and protected me and provided me with everything I needed. So did you. We don't have a fucking clue what it was like for her. I'm not going to judge her choice for not wanting to be vulnerable. I think she's wrong because she has so much to give. She'll be an amazing wife and mother. But I acknowledge it's her choice to make."

"What if you knew that a good guy wanted to love her and protect her and provide her with all she needed and she refused him?"

Matt looked at Adam and knew who that *good guy* was. "Adam. Have you told her?"

He shook his head. "I only just figured it out myself."

"Your last name may be Anderson but you really are a Lathem," Matt grinned. "We always figure it out before the women do. But that's a good thing," he added. "We get to prove to them that we deserve their trust and respect and their love."

"And will it work?"

"We're all happily married, aren't we?"

Adam couldn't argue with that.

15.

Pedicures… & More Prodding

Ella wanted a pedicure, so Katy declared a Spa Day. All the women, even the toddler women, would go into town and be pampered. Taxis were called and diaper bags were packed. Sophia and Lindsey were fortunately feeling well enough to join, so only men were left at home.

Maureen was thrilled with idea of three generations of Lathem women spending a few hours together and said so repeatedly on the drive to town and to the spa.

"When Shelby has a baby, we'll have four generations!" Maureen declared.

The statement had a duel effect on Shelby. She was pleased and grateful that Maureen considered her a grandchild. The Lathems had shown her nothing but love and kindness and treated her as Mark and Katy's daughter. But on the other hand, the idea that they were all waiting for her to settle down with a husband and children unnerved her. It wasn't exactly irritation, but more a feeling of knowing that she couldn't fulfill their desires and unable to vocalize her feelings. She'd tried with Adam and he hadn't understood. So Shelby just smiled and looked out of the window and waited for someone to change the subject.

The manager of the day spa greeted the three vans as they pulled up in front of the building. She remembered Janie and Ella from their past visits, a tradition for mother and daughter to have perfectly painted toes for the beach, and hurried the group inside where lemonade and piña coladas awaited. They would have to be divided into smaller groups to accommodate the large number of them, but within seconds the women had paired off with children included and the fun began.

Lindsey and Sophia and their three girls stood together in a group. Nic held Annie's hand, and Beth had Isabelle with her, promising Rory and Andrew she would never leave her eyesight. Maureen decided to join with them, leaving Katy, Janie, Ella and Shelby to form the last group. Shelby, watching Lindsey contend with her girls that were tired of standing still, took a step towards them.

"Why don't you and I be partners, Amanda? Will you help me pick out nail polish for my toes?" Shelby asked the four year old.

"I'd love to," Amanda beamed. "I know all my colors."

"Thank you," Lindsey mouthed as Shelby swooped up Amanda into her arms.

"We can take the girls while you're getting facials," Katy added.

"I think this is going to be fun," Sophia grinned as they were led off to the different areas of the spa.

As Janie and Katy settled in on the massage table, Ella on the table next to them, they both were thinking the same thing. Shelby had confided in Katy that she wasn't planning on having children, fearing her lack of maternal nature.

"She's convinced herself of something that isn't true," Katy frowned. "She will make a wonderful mother. She has a heart full of love just waiting to blanket another person with. Why can't she see it?"

Janie agreed. "I think it's fear. She's just scared. Maybe, when she realizes that, she'll be able to work through it. Sadly, we can't do it for her."

The massage therapists worked their magical hands up and down their backs and the muscle tension slowly oozed from their bodies, leaving them relaxed and refreshed.

"It will happen," Janie said as they wrapped themselves in the soft robes, ready for their facials. "I see in Adam's face a determination that wasn't there before. He has decided he wants something and I'm assuming it's Shelby," she shrugged. "You and I both know that there's nothing more persuasive than a Lathem man," she grinned.

"Let's hope so," Katy replied.

*****

Just like she'd offered, Shelby let Amanda pick out the polish that would be painted on her toes. Bright yellow would not have been her first choice, but Amanda was thrilled with it, so yellow it was. In fact, Amanda wanted them to match so they both ended up with neon yellow toenails.

They chatted away about Dora and The Little Mermaid and why her mommy didn't like bacon anymore. Shelby laughed as the conversation turned to her dad and how much hair he had on his face when he didn't shave. She didn't like it and Shelby had to agree. She preferred clean shaven men, too. She didn't like beards...not at all.

I've never seen Adam unshaven, she thought and somehow the thought gave her comfort. *He* had a beard...the bastard who'd almost killed her. No, Shelby didn't like beards either.

With the manicures completed and toenails painted, it was time for facials. All the children were ushered into the back where the manager had offered her two teenage daughters as babysitters. The moms eagerly accepted the generous offer, allowing all the women to enjoy quiet time as the pampering continued.

The conversation drifted to babies and motherhood, Beth asking question after question, unable to conceal her excitement and obvious inexperience.

"I don't feel any different," Beth said.

"Yet," Lindsey laughed.

"Thank your lucky stars," Sophia groaned.

"You poor thing," Janie sympathized. "You've had some rough pregnancies."

Sophia sighed. "You know, I remember being sick with Alex, but it didn't knock me out like this. Not that it would've mattered. I still would've had to work two jobs anyway."

"I can't even imagine," Janie frowned.

"Ben is wonderful though," Sophia grinned. "So considerate and thoughtful. And having mom and dad across the street helps, too. They love to come and play with Charlie and Lisa and give me a break. Although I'm always sick, I know I get a baby at the end, so I'm not going to complain *too* loudly," she grinned.

"I want to experience it all," Beth said wistfully. "This may be the only pregnancy I have so I want to treasure every minute of it."

Maureen smiled and patted her daughter-in-law's hand. "It took us almost five years to have Matthew. And then look what happened. Boom, boom, boom, boom! A total of seven and they came quickly," she chuckled. "Don't rule out anything. God has a plan for you, my dear. Just wait and see."

Shelby listened but didn't offer any pearls of wisdom from experience. She had no experience…no idea what they were all talking about. But she listened intently as all three pregnant women spoke with such love about a bunch of cells in their womb. They spoke of these cells as if they were already a child and completely head over heels in love with it. She didn't share her confusion. She just listened.

*****

The girls compared toenails as the taxis returned them to the estate. It had been a great way to spend a day and each of them had enjoyed it. The bond between these women was unbreakable. They were the best of friends and the closest of sisters, with Shelby accepted as one of their own.

She'd also enjoyed the day. She loved a day of pampering like the next woman, but she also loved the Lathem family, even though at times she thought they were all a bit crazy.

As the taxis pulled into the circular driveway and the men ran out to help everyone out of the cars and into the house, Shelby found herself with Adam at her arm.

"Have fun?" he grinned.

"I did," she smiled. "Amanda picked out my nail polish. Like it?" she asked as she lifted one of her feet and wiggled it in the air.

"Sexy," he winked. "*And*, you'll be able to jog in the dark."

"Ha ha," she grinned.

They walked into the house where kids were running everywhere and a steady hum of voices talking made it difficult to think.

"Wanna go for a walk?" she said, looking at Adam.

"Sure." He took her hand and led her through the great room and out the French doors that led to the walkway down to the beach. Several pairs of eyes watched them go.

Katy waved her arm to get Janie's attention and nodded in the direction of their kids. Janie smiled and hooked her arm through Matt's.

"Just let them find their own way," he whispered into her ear. It fell on deaf ears.

*****

"Can I ask you something?"

"Of course," Adam replied.

Shelby kept walking, kicking and splashing water with her feet as she went. It was several seconds before she asked her question.

"How soon do you feel the baby?"

"Huh?"

"When a woman is pregnant, how soon does she feel it?" she clarified. "I mean, I've been through medical school and I understand what happens and everything, but when do you *feel* it?"

"I'm not an OB," he prefaced with, "but I would suppose from everything I've seen, around eighteen weeks, give or take." When Shelby didn't respond, he added, "Why?"

"Oh, I'm not pregnant!" she gasped. "If that's what you were thinking."

"Okay."

"Just some of the stuff they were talking about today made me wonder."

They continued walking along the shore, the afternoon sun providing nourishment for the soul.

"Shelby, if I asked you to dinner, would you go?"

"Of course," she scoffed. "When have I turned down a free meal?" she joked.

"Shelby." Adam stopped walking and grabbed her arm. "Look at me."

She did.

"If I asked you to dinner…If I asked you on a date, would you go with me?"

"Why would you ask me on a date?" she whispered.

He stepped closer and moved a strand of hair caught in her eyelash. He gently tucked it behind her ear but didn't pull his hand away. Rather, he cupped her cheek and lowered his head 'til he was just inches from her face.

"Shelby," he whispered, and brushed his lips across hers for just a moment. "Would you have dinner with me?"

"Okay," she choked out.

"This evening?"

"Okay."

He brought his lips back to hers and pressed softly…a chaste kiss…gentle and sweet.

"Thank you," he smiled and stepped back. "You've made my day."

Taking her by the hand, he turned them around and headed back to the house. They walked in silence until they reached the screen doors.

"Seven?" he asked.

Shelby nodded and bit her bottom lip. Adam wondered if it was to hide a smile. He kissed her cheek and headed for the pool house. As she walked into the great room, Katy stood watching her, eyebrows raised.

"I won't be here for dinner," she said matter-of-factly.

"I'll let Cynthia know," Katy said.

"Thank you," replied Shelby as she dashed up the stairs.

*****

Soaking in the bath tub, Shelby let her mind wander back to the kiss on the beach. He'd startled her, but she'd liked it. For twelve years they'd been friends and now? She'd felt it the other day on the beach…when they were playing in the water. She'd wanted him to kiss her. The realization had come like a wave crashing over her that Adam was more than a friend…and had been for some time. She just couldn't admit it.

But now. Now he'd crossed the line. He'd kissed her and she'd wanted him to. Yet the fear of allowing someone to get close still persisted.

"But it's Adam," she said out loud. "He's already close."

Another realization. She slid down into the warm water, allowing it to cover her head. *It's just dinner!*

Drying herself and then her hair, Shelby took her time getting ready. She used lotion scented with vanilla and pear and rubbed it into her soft skin. She pulled a dress from a hanger hung on the bookshelf. It was a pale mint green halter dress that went half way down her thighs. She added wedges to her feet that showed off her marvelous yellow toenails. With her makeup expertly done, her hair cascading down her back, she was ready with fifteen minutes to spare. She grabbed her clutch and headed downstairs.

Before she hit the last step, the cat whistle made her look up. Mark and Peter sat on the leather sofa, both looking up at her and grinning.

"You are a gorgeous girl," Peter smiled. "If only I was fifty years younger."

Mark chuckled. "You do look beautiful, Shelby. Where are you off to?"

"Just into town for dinner," she smiled, blushing slightly.

"And what lucky young man gets to spend his evening with such a lovely young lady?" Maureen asked as she handed Peter a glass of water and then sat down beside him.

"That would be me!" Adam beamed as he entered the room through the open French doors.

"Well, that's…that's just wonderful!" Maureen replied,

obviously surprised at the revelation. "You two have a good time."

"We will," Adam grinned. "Ready?" he asked Shelby.

Shelby nodded and stepped off the last step and took his waiting hand.

"A woman who's ready early! How can I be so lucky?" he chuckled as he escorted her through the doors and onto the patio.

"Well look at you two!" Janie said, as they walked by her. "Have a great time."

They just smiled and kept walking.

16.

Dinner

"This is crazy!" Adam snorted as they stood waiting for the hostess to show them to their table.

"What?"

"How many meals have we eaten together?"

"I don't know," shrugged Shelby. "Hundreds?

"Exactly! So why am I nervous?" Adam chuckled.

Shelby was nervous too but she wasn't about to acknowledge it out loud. She just laughed at Adam and followed the hostess through the patio and to the corner table that overlooked the marina.

Adam held the chair for her and she smiled up at him, appreciating the gentlemanly gesture. The hostess handed them menus once Adam was also seated and then disappeared, leaving them alone. The sounds of the Caribbean, the metal drums, filled the air, as they watched two men a few hundred feet away playing for the tourists. The sun was slowly setting and the warm evening breeze fluttered the tablecloth.

Shelby glanced down at the menu as Adam placed their drink order from the bar. "Thank you," she smiled, Adam having ordered her favorite beer.

"I guess I should have asked you first. Sorry," he looked chagrinned.

Shelby chuckled. "Do I ever order anything else?"

"Well, no, but I should've asked."

"It's fine," she smiled. "I would've placed the same order."

The beers arrived, the waitress took their order and they sat in silence for a few minutes, watching the ocean. A young man, in his early teens, Adam guessed, approached their table with a basket of flowers.

"Buy your lady a flower?" he asked.

"I would love to buy my lady a flower," Adam grinned and pulled his wallet.

"Five dollars."

"Do you have change for a twenty?"

"No, but I'll give you four flowers," the boy grinned.

"Deal," Adam chuckled and pulled four roses from the basket and handed them to Shelby.

"Thank you," she smiled and inhaled the rich scent from the buds.

The young man turned and moved on to the next table.

"Oh, he's good," Shelby nodded as they heard the

people at the next table get the same line.

"I certainly don't mind buying four flowers for my lady. I should have bought the whole basket!"

"Adam," Shelby said.

"I know! You aren't my woman but we don't have to tell him that! It'll break his heart."

Shelby smiled again as the waitress arrived with the first course of a delicious meal.

*****

Pulling into the driveway, they could see a few lights still on in the house. Adam opened the door and Shelby slipped out of the car and they walked to the front door.

"I had a good time. Thank you," Shelby smiled.

"Thank you for accepting my invitation. Do you think, sometime, you'd have dinner with me again?"

"Maybe," she grinned. "We'll have to see what kind of mood I'm in when, and if, you ask me."

Adam laughed as he opened the door. They were met with laughter coming from the dining room. Following the noises, they found Tim and Beth, and Paul and Lindsey, and Andrew and Rory playing a card game, and obviously having a great time.

"Wanna join in?" Rory asked as he looked up to see them watching the chaos that was going on. Cards were being flung all over the table and there was a lot of cussing and swearing as well.

"Um, no thanks," said Shelby. "I have no idea what you guys are doing."

"NERTZ!!" screamed Lindsey, throwing her hands in the air and looking like she'd just won a gold medal.

Adam grinned and ushered Shelby to the kitchen. Opening the fridge, he pulled two bottles of water and handed one to Shelby. She took the bottle and said good night, leaving Adam alone. He wandered through the great room and out past the pool. Matt and his mom were swimming.

"Hey, honey," Janie smiled. "Have a good time."

"I think so," he said as he walked to the pool house. "Goodnight."

Janie looked at Matt and began to say something.

"Nope!" he said, shaking his head. "Leave it. He'll work it out."

Janie sighed. "I guess you might be right."

"Huh?"

"I said I guess you might be right," she repeated.

"Huh?" he said again.

"Very funny!" she pouted, but couldn't hide the grin that was forming.

Matt swam close to her and pulled her into his arms. "Stop thinking about the needs of your son and think about the needs of your husband. I'm *very* needy," he winked.

"Yes, you are."

Adam watched his parents in the pool as he closed the curtains. They were like teenagers when they were alone. They couldn't keep their hands off each other. He'd seen the way Matt looked at his mom. It was a love so intense there was no way to hide it. All of the brothers had the same look. They loved their wives with a passion that was undeniable to anyone who knew them…or even just saw them.

It's what he wanted…for himself and for his wife.

*****

It was another glorious day in the Bahamas. A week had passed and in six days they would be returning home. But that meant that they still had six days to play and relax.

As usual, mornings brought chaos in the house. Breakfast was always crazy. Kids were running and screaming, playing and laughing, crying and whining. Ben and Paul attempted to catch up on work emails and make any necessary calls, and Sophia spent most of the time running back and forth to the bathroom.

Shelby hadn't come downstairs yet and there was no sign of Tim and Beth. Nic and Maureen were huddled in the corner of the kitchen when Janie joined them. Within a minute or two, the group broke up and Janie walked straight to Adam and said, "I need you upstairs."

He followed, worried. When they reached the second floor, and far away from everyone, Janie turned to her son, a concerned expression on her face. "Can you please go and talk to Beth? She's in her room. She's had some spotting and is absolutely beside herself."

"I'm not an OB but I can certainly talk to her," he replied immediately and hurried down the hall. He knocked on the door and entered to find Beth sobbing, almost hysterically on the bed.

"Hey, hey," Adam soothed and rushed to her side.

"I can't lose this baby," she cried. "I just can't!"

"Okay," Adam said. "Tell me what's going on."

Ten minutes later, Adam exited the room and went to find Matt. He needed to borrow the car. He'd decided it was necessary that Beth go to the hospital. It was probably nothing, but he couldn't be sure.

"Of course!" Matt replied.

Five minutes later, Adam was behind the wheel with Tim and Beth in the backseat and they were pulling onto the main road.

*****

Shelby hadn't been able to fall asleep so when the sunlight had streamed through the window, she'd gotten up and closed the curtains and gone back to bed.

She liked Adam, she really did, perhaps too much. But it was becoming *way* too complicated. They were friends. Good friends, but just friends. It had to be *only* friends. She couldn't handle anything more than that.

Unable to sleep any longer, she figured she may as well get up. She needed to talk to Adam, no matter how uncomfortable the conversation was going to be. She needed him to know that they couldn't be anything more than friends. She'd made the decision years ago. She just had to stick to it no matter how conflicted she was feeling.

Finishing quickly in the bathroom, Shelby bounded down the stairs and into the kitchen. Within a few seconds, the somber mood told her something was wrong.

"What's going on?" she asked Katy.

"Beth is bleeding. Adam's taken her to the hospital."

"Oh, no," Shelby whispered, her heart breaking. "When will we know anything?"

"They only left about thirty minutes ago, so not for a while."

Shelby poured herself a cup of coffee and walked over to the small desk that had the computer. Sitting down, she watched the women trying to keep their emotions in check, a task most difficult. Most of the children had been taken to play outside, leaving the women to fret in peace.

Opening up her email, Shelby tried to busy herself so she wouldn't have to think about the possibility of Beth losing her baby. She imagined it would be devastating. Deleting junk mail and skipping over credit card statements, she came to one that she'd been waiting for. With her finger on the mouse, she opened the email and held her breath. Scanning quickly through the words on the screen, she silently screamed. She now knew where she would be spending the next four years of her life.

17.

Surprises

Beth chewed on her fingernails, a habit she'd picked up only a couple of hours earlier that very morning. Lying in a hospital gown with Tim by her side holding her hand, they waited as the technician hooked up the ultrasound machine. It appeared to be a very complicated process, one that Tim joked, trying to lighten the mood, they should probably get used to.

Adam had been in communication with Beth's doctor, Dr. Ringer in New York, and between the three of them, the attending doctor at the hospital included, they knew how to proceed. The Fetal Doppler had picked up something, but inconclusive, so the next test would be a vaginal ultrasound.

"I'll leave," Adam said.

"No!" Beth grabbed his arm. "I need you to stay."

Adam nodded and pulled up a stool and sat next to her, holding her hand, with Tim on the other side of the gurney. They all watched as the technician squeezed gel onto the end of the probe and then, smiling at Beth, lifted the sheet and began the procedure.

"Breath normally," she said, noting Beth holding her breath. "Am I hurting you?"

Beth shook her head. Undergoing years of fertility treatments had left her almost numb to the poking and prodding of doctors and nurses. This was certainly nothing worse than anything she'd been through. In fact, it wasn't even the first time she'd been subjected to this same machine.

After several minutes, doing all kinds of thing on the machine that Beth had no understanding of, the kind woman patted Beth on the knee and said, "I need to go and talk to the doctor and we'll be right back, okay?"

Beth nodded and as soon as the door had closed she turned to Adam, panic written all over her face. "What's wrong? Tell me what you see!"

"This is not my area of expertise, Beth."

"But you know something! I see it in your face!"

Adam tried to remain blank in his expression, but he needed to tell her *something*. It wasn't fair to leave her so panicked. He couldn't be entirely sure of what he saw on the computer screen but he had a pretty good idea. "I see a strong heartbeat," he smiled.

"You do?"

"I do," he confirmed. "Now, let's wait for the doctor, ok?"

*****

The Lathem women remained vigilant in their worry. Huddled in the kitchen, the tension was so thick it could be cut with the proverbial knife. The men, although also concerned, stayed outside on the beach with all the children, knowing that standing and wringing their hands would do nothing to help and accomplish nothing.

Shelby was anxious for Beth. She'd seen the heartache infertility had brought to her life and wished her well. But the clinical side of her brain seemed to win the battle in her head as she watched the nervous fidgeting and useless chatter that filled the room.

There's no point to all of this, she thought. *It isn't as though all their worrying and stressing is going to help Beth in any possible way.* "Why don't you all sit down and I'll make another pot of coffee," she suggested.

Nods and mumbles of agreement ensued and within seconds, Shelby was filling the pot with water and pulling cups for the cupboard.

"I just can't even imagine," Janie said. "It must be agonizing for her."

Lindsey nodded. "It's the worst moment in the world. So helpless to do anything even though it's your own body."

"And it's not as if she hasn't already bonded with that baby," added Sophia.

"Huh?" Shelby was shocked. "How? She only found out she was pregnant a couple of days ago."

All eyes swung to her and she suddenly felt stupid for voicing her thoughts. But the response was in no way harsh.

Janie smiled and nodded. "I know, but...I haven't met a woman who hasn't instantly fallen in love with their baby the second they found out it existed. When I was pregnant with the boys, I would sit and rub my tummy and sing to them and talk to them like they were sitting on my lap. And Matt did the same thing with Ella and Christopher. He would kneel down and kiss my belly, believing that somehow that emotion and love was being felt by his child still safely inside me."

"Paul did the same thing," smiled Nic, recalling the memories. "Actually, the last few weeks before Gregory was born, he read *all* the Harry Potter books to him," she chuckled.

The woman laughed, knowing that their own husbands had done much the same thing, Sophia adding, "Ben tells this one to stop making mommy so sick," she said as she rubbed her growing belly.

Shelby was mystified by the conversation around her and her face obviously showed it.

"It all seems so strange to you, I know," Maureen smiled. "But one day when you find out you're pregnant, you'll completely understand."

Once again, Shelby decided to keep the thoughts running through her mind to herself.

*****

"Holy shit!" Tim exclaimed. "Are you sure?"

"We can see here, here, and here, three distinct heart beats."

"Three," Beth whispered. "Three?"

"Three," Adam confirmed. "Not necessarily unheard of in IVF pregnancies. I have several sets of twins and a set of triplets as patients."

"Well, add another set," Tim beamed.

"I'd be honored," Adam smiled.

The doctor left the examination room to call Beth's doctor in New York, Adam following behind him, leaving Beth to get dressed.

Tim couldn't stop grinning. "Three babies! Wow! When we do something, we go all out, don't we?"

Beth seemed to still be in a state of shock. "Three," she said again. "Three!"

"Let's help you up and back into your clothes," Tim said as he pulled the sheet from her legs and moved around the bed to grab her clothes that were lying on the chair. He gently helped her to a sitting position and untied the gown at the back. "Okay, arms up," he ordered.

Beth obeyed, her mind still on the fact that there were three babies growing inside her.

"Right arm," Tim said. "Good girl. Left arm."

A few minutes later they emerged from the room, Adam waiting with a wheelchair.

"I don't need that," Beth stated, but Tim guided her to the chair and forced her into it.

"Get used to it," he grinned. "I assume triplets is considered a complicated pregnancy?"

Adam nodded. "Your doctor will be sending you an email this afternoon with some instructions and you'll need to see him as soon as you get home."

"Do we need to leave early?" Tim asked. "Today?"

Adam smiled. "No. Beth needs to take it easy…very easy…and she *and* the babies will be just fine, although it's still very early, so you don't want to take any unnecessary risks."

"No! No risks!" Beth agreed.

*****

The news of triplets was welcomed with shouts of joy and complete surprise. An impromptu party ensued with dancing and champagne, none of either for Beth, however. But she didn't mind. All but swaddled in a blanket and carried to the couch by her doting husband, Beth's heart was overflowing as her hands unconsciously lay across her stomach, protecting and guarding the precious babies growing inside her.

Shelby came and sat beside her and gave her a hug. "I'm glad you're okay. Everyone here was going out of their minds with worry."

Beth sighed. "Me, too. After all these years to finally be pregnant and then…well…thinking that it was all over before it had really even started. I've never been as scared in my whole life."

"Can I touch your babies?" Amanda asked, as she came and stood in front of Beth.

"They're still in my tummy," Beth replied. "And they won't come out for a long time, but you can touch them when they do."

Shelby chuckled as Amanda skipped off happily. "And to think, you're going to have three of those!"

Beth smiled. "Yep! And I'll do anything...*everything* it takes to get them here safely. You know, I made a deal with God this morning. I told him that if one of us had to die, I'd prefer it be me. I love this baby, well, *babies*, with all my heart and I'd gladly give up my life if it means they're healthy. Gladly!"

The statement shocked Shelby. "But if you die, they die, too. That makes no sense."

"Well, yes, technically that's true," Beth grinned. "But the fact is, I get it. Loving someone so much that you would risk your life bringing them into the world. No questions."

Tim arrived with a plate of food for his wife. Shelby hugged Beth again, told her again how happy she was for them, and left an empty place for Tim to claim and sit next to Beth. She wandered out to the pool and beyond to the garden.

"What a concept!" she said to herself as she stepped on the rock pathway that led to a small wrought iron bench. *A mother would be willing to risk her life to protect her child.* She'd had no such mother. Yet, here she was, in a family where the concept was the norm. Anatomy classes, biology, neuroscience, and pathology lab had done nothing to educate her in the ways of a mother's heart. "I'm at a disadvantage," she muttered to herself. "I have no personal experience here."

"Personal experience in what?"

The voice startled her, making her jump.

"Adam! Don't sneak up on me like that! You're gonna give me a heart attack!"

"Sorry," he grinned. "I wasn't trying to surprise you."

"I was just thinking."

"I heard. What don't you have experience in?"

"A mother's love."

"Well, technically no, but you certainly have the instincts."

She swung to look at him, irritation in her expression. "There is no way that you can know that!" she snapped.

"Of course there is."

"Don't be ridiculous."

Adam, deciding not to rile her any further, changed the subject. "Mom needs me to run to the store to get more milk. These kids are drinking gallons a day! Come with me."

18.

Maternal Instinct

"Do we need a cart?" Shelby asked.

"The kids are drinking five gallons of milk a day!" Adam replied. "I'm going to get ten this time."

Wandering down the aisle to the back of the store and the dairy section, Shelby saw a young boy standing alone just a few feet in front of them.

"Hi, honey," she said as she crouched in front of him. "Where's your mommy?"

The little boy, Shelby guessed to be about five years old, just looked up at her with big brown eyes and shrugged.

"Would you like me to help you find her?"

He nodded. Shelby took his small hand in hers and turned to Adam. He smiled. Heading back the way they'd come, Shelby and the boy walked towards the cashiers.

"Oh my goodness! There you are, Israel! You scared me!" A young woman ran towards them and dropped to her knees, sweeping the boy into her arms. "Thank you so much for finding him," she said to Shelby. "Thank you."

"No problem," Shelby smiled. She said goodbye to

Israel and headed to find Adam, who was filling the grocery cart with milk. "He's safely back with his mom," she announced stopping in front of the dairy case.

"Good. He looked scared to death."

"I know, my heart broke when I looked into those big brown eyes," Shelby frowned.

They pushed the cart back down the aisle and paid for the ten gallons of milk. On the way to the car in the parking lot, they watched Israel and his mother walking away, hand in hand.

"You did a great thing back there," Adam smiled.

"Someone would've found him. He was just standing there. It's not like he was hiding or anything."

"No, but he obviously trusted you."

"Yes, he did."

As they rode back to the house, Shelby thought about those big brown eyes and how relieved his mother looked when she saw him walking towards her. She was glad she could help. When they arrived home, they unloaded the milk from the trunk of the car and hauled it all into the kitchen.

"Thank so much," Katy smiled, as she put a few of the gallons into the fridge, the others needing to go in the fridge in the pantry. "This should keep the little rug rats going for a little while," she said as he winked at Janie.

"Yes," Janie agreed. "It should do for a day or two."

*****

That evening, Cynthia was grilling chicken for dinner. Maureen had suggested they eat outside, too. The kids were loud as they played and Janie and Katy were carrying silverware and plates from the kitchen.

"Can I help?" Shelby offered.

"Sure," Janie replied. "Can you grab the tray of condiments? It's next to the fridge."

Shelby headed through the French doors and into the great room. There stood Annie trying to lift one of the stools at the island.

"Whatcha doing there?" Shelby asked.

"This has to go on here," Annie frowned.

"On where?" Shelby asked.

"Here!" Annie demanded, pointing to another stool.

As Shelby walked up to Annie, still struggling with the weight of the stool, she asked, "Why?"

"Can you help me?"

"Okay," Shelby answered, unsure of what the three year old was actually trying to accomplish. She lifted the stool from the ground and stacked it on top of the other stool. "Now what?"

"Now this stool has to go on there." She was pointing

to a third stool.

"Are we making a tower?"

"Yes!" Annie exclaimed, delighted with the plan.

"Why?"

"So I can touch the ceiling."

"Oh, of course," Shelby grinned. "Silly me." But looking up at the ten foot ceilings, she knew it was going to take many more stools than were in the kitchen at present. "Um, what if we do it another way?" she offered.

"How?" asked Annie, skeptical of a plan other than her own.

"Well," said Shelby, as she lifted Annie and sat her on the island. "What if," she said as she jumped onto the island, too, "I stand up here," she said as she stood, "and lift you up like this?" She lifted Annie into her arms, careful of the two pendants lights hanging from the ceiling, and maneuvered Annie into the air. Annie stretched her arms and then with a tiny 'thud' hit the ceiling with her hand.

"YAY!!" she exclaimed, as Shelby pulled her down to her chest and held her firmly.

"What are you doing?" Adam asked as he strolled into the kitchen.

"Touching the ceiling," replied Shelby, as if it was the most natural thing in the world.

"I touched the ceiling, Adam!" Annie grinned.

"I saw you," Adam answered. "It's time for dinner. Want some chicken?"

"Yes, I do!" Annie declared.

Shelby handed her down to Adam who placed her on the floor and she skipped off outside for dinner. Shelby stepped to the edge of the counter and Adam reached for her and helped her down, her body sliding down his as her feet stretched for the floor. For a split second, their entire bodies were touching and the awareness of her filled every one of his senses. Before he was able to do something stupid, Shelby stepped away.

"So...was that your idea?" he chuckled.

Shelby laughed as she walked over to the stools, still stacked together. "No. I came in and she was trying to build a tower so she could touch the ceiling. I figured a controlled environment was probably the best way to give her what she wanted."

"Good idea," agreed Adam. "That girl is fearless and there's no telling what stunt she would have come up with to achieve her goal." *And you don't think you'd be a great mother?* Adam was convinced of how wonderful she really would be.

*****

The next morning the sound of a car pulling into the driveway caused Adam to alter his route to the kitchen. He wandered down the hall and opened the front door. A young woman, in her twenties and blonde, bounded up to the stairs and stopped a few feet in front of him.

"Good morning, Sir. I am here to see Mrs. Elizabeth Lathem. I'm here from the hospital to check on her."

"Hi," he smiled. "Come on in." She followed behind him as he walked into the small reception room off the hall. "If you'd like to wait here, I'll go and find her."

She nodded and stood in the middle of the room.

"Make yourself comfortable," he offered and left her as he went in search of Beth.

Adam finally found her still in her room and she and Tim quickly made their way down the stairs and off to see the nurse.

"Who's that?" Tyler asked Adam.

"Someone from the hospital. She's here to do a quick check-up on Beth."

"She's totally hot!" Tyler smiled.

"Is she?" Adam asked.

"Oh, come on!" Tyler laughed. "She's totally your type. Don't tell me you didn't notice."

Adam grinned. "I noticed."

"So, you gonna ask her out?"

"I don't even know her name!"

"So?"

"Oh, right," Adam grinned. "I forgot who I was talking to for a second there."

"So…are you?"

"I…ah…well…"

"Are you?" Shelby asked, as she walked down the stairs.

Adam's head whipped around to see her, her expression serious, her brows slightly lifted.

"No. I'm not."

"Well, if she's totally hot, why not?" Shelby asked, eyebrows raised.

"Because I'm not interested in *her*."

"So, you don't care if I, uh, walk her out?" Tyler asked.

"No, I don't care," Adam frowned.

Tyler left Adam to go and hover by the doorway to make his move when she was finished with Beth.

"Don't do anything on my account," Shelby said as she came to the last step, just a couple of feet from Adam.

"I won't."

Shelby drifted past him, her chin a little too high, her

expression a little too tight.

She's jealous! He grinned.

*****

"Everything looks good, Mrs. Lathem. The doctor wanted me to give you these vitamins and you're gonna follow up with your doctor when you get back to New York, right?"

"Right," nodded Tim. "We've already made the appointment."

"Good," she nodded. "Hopefully, you won't need to come back and see us, but if you're at all worried, you come right in, okay?"

"Thank you," smiled Beth. "We will."

Suddenly Tyler was there to walk the young lady out to her car, leaving Tim and Beth alone.

"I will not do anything to risk these babies," Beth said. "I will climb into a bubble wrapped room for the next seven or eight months if that's what it takes."

Tim chuckled. "I don't think we have to go to that extreme, but taking it easy is definitely a must."

And they sat, side by side, rubbing Beth's still very flat tummy.

19.

Realization

Shelby stomped along the sand, kicking at the water every so often as it rippled over her toes. "He can damn well go out with anyone he wants to!" she muttered. "Oooh, she's totally hot!" she mimicked Tyler. "Well, go out with her then!" she continued her ranting. Fortunately there was nobody around to hear her.

After walking for several minutes, the tirade finally wore thin and a sense of calm returned. She turned around and retraced her steps back towards the house, stopping a hundred yards or so before the gate to the garden. Flopping down onto the sand, she looked up at the blue sky overhead. Laying back, she placed her arm over eyes, shielding herself from the bright sun glaring down on her.

She'd only been there for a few minutes when she heard someone sit next to her.

"May I join you?" Katy asked.

"I'm not doing anything," Shelby replied, with a hint of sarcasm in her voice, but feeling relief it was only Katy interrupting her solitude.

"Well I don't want to do anything either," Katy laughed. "That's why I want to join you." She sat down in the warm sand. "You okay?"

"Why wouldn't I be?"

"Because I watched you stomping down the beach like you were about to kill something, or someone."

"Nope! I'm just dandy."

The tone of her voice said otherwise, but Katy let it go. "It's been a weird week. Saying goodbye to Ray was...*is* hard. And then Beth and Tim's news is so exciting."

"And then there's my news," Shelby said.

"What news?"

"I got the email the other day. *The* email," she repeated.

"What?" Katy exclaimed. "Why didn't you tell me? Say something?"

"With Beth and everything I...well, I didn't want to rain on her parade." Shelby sat up and brushed the sand from her legs.

"Oh, Shelby! There is plenty of joy to go around. So? Where are you going?"

"I'm not *going* anywhere. Isn't that exciting?"

"Huh? I don't get it." Katy swung around to face her.

"I'm staying in New York," she grinned. "Mount Sinai."

"Holy shit! That's fantastic," Katy screamed and pulled

Shelby into a hug. "We have to...you have to tell everyone!"

"When there's nothing else going on."

"There's nothing else going on," Katy declared, as she climbed to her feet, dragging Shelby with her.

And so another party took place on the patio of the Lathem estate that evening. Pulling out all the stops, the family danced and partied 'til almost midnight in celebration of the wonderful news. Many family members expressed relief, now knowing that Shelby wouldn't be leaving the city.

"You realize I'll be working one hundred hours a week," she chuckled when Derek had talked about being able to continue his relentless teasing of his surrogate little sister.

"Yep, you will be," Adam agreed with a smile. "But it's all worth it in the end."

Slowly, couple by couple, the family disappeared, calling it a night and returning to their rooms. It was just after one o'clock when the only ones left were Shelby and Adam. "Well, goodnight," she said as she went to stand.

Adam grabbed her arm, forcing her to remain seated beside him. "Why didn't you tell me?" he asked, the hurt obvious in his voice.

Shelby shrugged. "There was so much with Beth and triplets and...and stuff. I didn't want to ruin her moment."

"But why didn't you tell *me*?" he repeated.

She looked down at her hands fidgeting in her lap. The truth was, she was going to tell him earlier that very morning, but as she'd come down the stairs she heard him and Tyler talking about how hot the nurse was and she'd changed her mind. "I didn't think you'd care," trying to sound nonchalant in her reply. But even as she heard the words, it just sounded immature. *Am I still in middle school?* She rolled her eyes.

"You know that's crap," he called her out.

"Yeah," she admitted. "I just hadn't found the right time."

Adam swung around to face her, placing his hand on her thigh, his thumb lightly caressing the soft skin of her leg. "Shelby," he whispered.

"Can't sleep. Gonna go for a swim. You guys wanna come in?" Tyler interrupted as he wandered out to the pool. He threw a towel on an empty chair and dove in to the cool water.

Livid with his brother, Adam stood, grabbed Shelby's hand and dragged her around the pool and into the pool house, closing the door behind him. He pulled the curtains closed and turned on the lamp next to the bed, emitting a soft glow over the room. "Have a seat," he instructed as he walked to the fridge and pulled two bottles from the shelves in the door. "Beer?" he asked. Shelby shook her head. Adam popped off both tops anyway and went and sat next to her on the small sofa.

"I figured you already knew, but I guess I should say it out loud and tell you."

"What?' she asked.

Adam took a long drink, stifled a burp and then said, "I have feelings for you, Shelby. I have for a long time."

As Shelby began to speak, he threw his hands up in to the air. "I don't want you to say anything until you've heard me out."

She closed her mouth.

"Over the past few years we've spent a lot of time together," he continued. "I guess, at first, we ended up together at family parties and stuff because we were close in age and had medicine in common. And we did...we do. And what may have started out as just a mutual interest, well, for me, has grown into much more. I like to spend time with you. I *want* to spend time with you. You are the last person I think about before falling asleep at night and the first person I think about when I wake up in the morning. And many nights I dream about you, too. Of all the people in the world, you are the one I couldn't live without."

As he took a breath, Shelby looked up at his face and their eyes met. He knew in that moment that she felt the same way, too. He knew beyond doubt that she was his future. Somehow he needed to convince her that she knew it, too.

"I love you, Shelby. I don't expect you to say anything, I just want you to know that I love you and that I'll do whatever you want or need me to do to make you happy. I see us growing old together, spending our lives laughing and loving and making a home and having a family."

He saw it instantly...the panic that rose through her entire body. It was too much for her. She stood.

"No! Don't go! I didn't mean to...to scare you. We can take it as slow as you need." Her shoulders dropped a fraction and he heard her exhale slowly. "I mean it," he said. I'll do anything you need. I am yours to command."

The faintest of smiles crossed her lips. "You shouldn't give me that kind of power. You might just live to regret it."

"Never," he exclaimed as he stood and faced her, their bodies almost touching. "Shelby, I've never told a woman I loved them. I've never felt this way about anyone. It's almost frightening but it's a good frightening," he smiled.

"That doesn't even make sense."

"I know, but it's how I feel." Adam lifted his hand and gently cupped her cheek, then cautiously bent his head to hers and lightly pressed his lips to hers.

Closing her eyes, Shelby accepted the sweet kiss, but as Adam unconsciously pressed closer and nipped her bottom lip with his teeth, she stepped back and out of his reach. Then she turned and left him alone as she walked out of the pool house, around the pool and into the main house. He wanted to run after her, to make her stay and talk out her fears, but he knew she needed time...time to digest his revelation, and time to realize she loved him, too.

*****

Although he'd never said anything before tonight,

Shelby knew that her relationship with Adam was more than just friends. As he'd said the words, they were somehow familiar to her, with her feeling the same way. Hearing Adam say it aloud, though, had made everything real and no longer deniable.

Adam was the last person she thought about at night. He was the first person she thought of in the morning. When something good happened, he was the first person she wanted to tell. When something not-so-good happened, he was also the first one she thought of.

But it was all different now. He'd laid his cards on the table and their relationship was forever changed. Unfamiliar territory was where she found herself, floating adrift in a sea of emotion. Emotions that ranged from flattered and validated as a woman, to terrified and confused.

After several hours of tossing and turning, dozing on and off, still tired but morning upon her, Shelby dressed and headed downstairs to the waiting bedlam for a cup of coffee. Amazingly enough, Ella and Cynthia were the only ones in the kitchen.

"Coffee, Miss Shelby?" asked Cynthia.

"Yes, please," Shelby replied, slipping onto a stool next to Ella.

Placing the cream and sugar in front of her, Cynthia smiled as she slid the cup of coffee to Shelby and asked if she'd like some breakfast.

Shelby smiled and declined. "Where is everyone? Are we the first ones up?"

"Good gracious, no!" Cynthia laughed. It's almost ten o'clock."

"What?" Shelby was stunned.

"You slept in," Ella stated.

"I guess I did."

"Shelby, are you and Adam going to get married?"

She choked on the mouthful of coffee, sending her into a coughing fit. Finally, regaining control of her lungs, she wiped the tears than had run down her cheeks, and noticed Ella was still waiting patiently for an answer.

"Well?"

"Why would you ask me that?" Shelby inquired, curious what the answer would be.

"Mom and Katy were talking at the spa."

"And? What did they say?"

"Adam has decided he wants you, but you're too scared and they hope you can figure it all out because you'd make a wonderful mother."

"Did they now?" Shelby didn't know whether to be livid or amused. Deciding not to let the conversation go any further, she excused herself and walked up the staircase to take a shower.

*****

Adam had been sitting by the pool waiting for a glimpse of Shelby. He didn't want to pressure her but he needed to see how she would react to him the morning after his honest declaration. Would she avoid him? Would it be awkward between them? He only had four days until they returned to New York and back to the hustle and bustle of regular life. He wanted to know where he stood before they boarded the plane for home. He wanted to know if she could take a leap of faith and trust him with her heart. The waiting was killing him and after an hour, there was still no sign of her.

Strolling through the French doors into the house, he found Ella and Cynthia rolling out dough on the granite counter. "Cookies?" he smiled.

"Pie," Ella answered.

"Yum," Adam replied. "Have you seen Shelby?"

"Upstairs, Mr. Adam," Cynthia said, never taking her eyes of the dough being stretched under her deft hand.

"Thanks," and he headed for the stairs. Taking two at a time, he reached the door of the music room before he had a chance to formulate in his mind what he was going to say. But it wouldn't have mattered anyway because the moment he saw her step from the bathroom, wrapped in a towel, her wet hair clinging her shoulders, his mind went completely blank. He was unable to form one coherent thought.

He silently chastised his behavior. Three days ago, Shelby walking from the bathroom wrapped in a towel still would have stirred his insides, but wouldn't have made him tongue tied like the long ago days of middle school.

"Uh, hi," he stammered. She smiled and his knees weakened. He mentally cursed each one individually. "Uh, I'll let you get dressed and then would you like to take a walk with me?"

"I'll meet you downstairs."

Adam nodded and left her as she entered her bedroom and shut the door behind her. "I'm a pathetic moron," he muttered as he stepped off the bottom stair and walked down the hall to the library.

"I'll second that," Derek laughed.

Adam smirked. "Thanks."

"What's wrong with you?"

"I'm successful, not a bad looking doctor. I should have all the confidence in the world."

"And you don't?"

"Nope. Not when it comes to…well…nope."

"Shelby?" Derek grinned.

"What? Why would you…huh?"

"Oh, come on!" Derek laughed. "It's not like I don't know."

"But, how? I only found out a few days ago."

Derek shook his head as they walked into the library and sat in two brown leather wingback chairs. "I know that we don't talk much, other than about sports and stuff, but can I give you a piece of advice?" Adam nodded, so Derek continued. "She's pretty much been my sister for the past twelve years and while we've never lived under the same roof for more than a few days at a time, I've gotten to know her pretty well. As awkward as it is to say, she likes you. You're the only man she looks at as a *man*."

"Huh?"

"Well, there's family and then there's the opposite sex...and she looks at me, and Mark, and Matt and all the Lathem males as family. But you? You're a man."

"You're full of it, and this is...is a very awkward conversation," Adam frowned.

"Maybe I'm not explaining it well, but, trust me, she has feelings for you and if you hurt her, I'll beat the shit out of you." The tone of Derek's voice had Adam understanding he was deadly serious.

"I'm not planning on hurting her. I'm planning on marrying her."

"Oh." Derek's eyes widened. "Well, okay then."

*****

Shelby had dressed and headed back to the bathroom to blow dry her hair. She'd taken her time, not purposely making him wait...well...maybe. With the large round brush she aimed the hair dryer at each section of hair and meticulously styled it into big wavy curls...stalling if she were to be honest with herself. When she had no other reason to be upstairs, she slowly made her way down to the great room, as the family was gradually starting to gather, their stomachs reminding them it was lunch time.

Salad and soup with Panini sandwiches were spread over the kitchen island, with mothers plating food for their children. The men stood in small clusters, patiently waiting for their turn to pile their plates high with the fuel that would keep them playing all afternoon on the beach; building sand castles, swimming, and some beach volleyball or football, possibly both.

With the children happily eating, and most of the women congregating with plates balancing on their laps on the massive sectional sofa in the great room, Shelby watched as Peter led the male assault on the kitchen. But mostly, she watched Adam. He was talking to Tim as they scooped up the spinach salad and piled it on their plates. She hadn't made eye contact with him yet – there were too many people blocking any possible interaction. She sat in a chair by the doors that led to the pool. Janie and Maureen were sitting close by, engrossed in a conversation about planning another family cruise the following year, so she just watched Adam as he sat at the table and ate his lunch, unaware of her across the room and the battle her emotions were waging.

As she'd stood in the shower earlier that morning, the realization came that she'd longed for a partner, an equal, a soul mate. The knowledge that Adam was offering a long-buried desire had emotions bubbling to the surface that she was sure she'd rid herself of years before. At the ripe old age of fourteen, Shelby had made some life decisions that she hadn't questioned once…until last night.

She didn't hate men, although she had good reason to, but she was wary of most of them and never allowed herself to be in *any* situation where she might be made to feel vulnerable. She didn't criticize marriage, although she'd decided it would never be for her, and she knew many couples, especially Katy and Mark, who were deeply in love and had made it a successful institution. She didn't ridicule motherhood, even though she knew, without question, that she would never have a child, and was genuinely grateful to the Lathem women who trusted her with their children, giving her an opportunity to rock a baby to sleep and play dolls and build Lego spaceships, time she truly treasured. She had never put herself in a situation where she'd questioned her resolve…until now.

20.

Possibility

It wasn't on purpose, but somehow Shelby and Adam's paths hadn't crossed 'til late afternoon. The men had played football on the beach and Shelby had been roped into going into town shopping with several of the women and a few of the children. By the time they returned, the afternoon was almost gone and it was time to think about dinner preparations.

A tradition at the Lathem vacation home was what Christopher called Garden Movie Night. Matt and Bob had constructed a pulley system to hoist a white screen into the air at one end of the lawn, allowing the family to lay on pillows and blankets and watch a movie in the lush garden after the sun had set. Christopher had reminded his father while on the beach earlier in the day that they had yet to enjoy the family ritual on this trip. "Okay," Matt had agreed. "Tonight, then." He and Bob had spent the better part of an hour rigging up the screen and hauling the sound system from the storage room to the garden and Adam had offered to help running wires for the speakers.

"Shelby?" Janie called through the great room. "Would you please run these out to Matt?"

Happy to help, Shelby left the little girls playing Candy Land on the floor and took the pliers from Janie and headed through the French doors, around the side of the house to the lawn area designated for movie watching.

Spotting Matt crouched in front of a speaker, she handed him the pliers. He looked up at her with confusion in his eyes.

"Janie said you needed these," she explained.

To the left of Shelby, a movement caught Matt's eye. Adam! *Nicely done, Janie.* He was impressed with his wife's *prodding* skills, even though he didn't actually approve of her meddling. *Okay, I'll play along.* He stifled a grin. "I think Adam needs them."

"Oh, right," Shelby replied, unaware of the scheming that had taken place in the kitchen, and now in the garden. She walked over the green grass to where Adam sat attaching wires to the back of a stereo receiver. "Here," she said and offered him the tool in her hand.

Adam looked at the pliers and then up to Shelby. "And I need those, why?"

Shelby shrugged. "Your mom said to bring them out and Matt told me to give them to you."

"Oh, well, thank you, then," he said as he took them from her and placed them on the ground beside him. After a moment or two of silence, he asked, "Do you know what movie the kids have picked?"

"The girls want Tangled and Joseph has the Cars Blu-ray in his hand and is refusing to put it down, so I'm thinking that one just might be the winner," she smiled.

Adam chuckled. "Probably. How was your trip into town?"

Shelby sighed. "I know that women are supposed to like shopping, but, I just don't get a kick out of it like everyone else. Although I did find a couple of things that I ended up buying."

"Like what?"

"A swimming suit and a sarong."

"We'll have to go swimming then so you can wear it before we head home."

Shelby smiled. "I think that can be arranged."

Adam finished plugging in all the speaker wires to the back of the receiver and turned it on to test it. As each speaker came to life, the set-up was complete. "I do believe we are ready for the Lathem Garden Movie Night," he grinned.

"You didn't need the pliers?"

*****

"We should draw straws," Nic repeated. "It's the only way it's going to be fair."

"But if Dad wins, we'll be watching an ancient John Wayne movie," whined Tim.

"And if Sophia wins, it'll be anything with Daniel Craig in it," Ben teased his wife.

"That's better than a Jane Austen movie," Matt chimed in. "And we know if Janie wins that's what it'll be."

"Just get the damn straws," Peter interrupted.

Mark jumped up and rummaged through the kitchen draws 'til he found some wooden skewers. Snipping one so it was considerably shorter than the others, he gathered them in his hands and headed back to the adults, each pulling a straw from the cluster he held tightly in his fist.

"This is a ridiculous way to choose a movie," Maureen muttered as she took a skewer from her son. "Damn!" she frowned as she pulled out a long one, knowing her choice of Breakfast at Tiffany's was now out of the running.

By the time all the skewers were picked, it was Rory who'd won the right to select the movie the adults would watch after the children went to bed.

"Oh, God knows what he's going to pick," sighed David. Matt and Paul muttered in agreement, suddenly not very excited at the prospect of watching a movie under the stars.

Rory, however, was gleefully jumping around announcing to everyone that he'd won, as if they didn't already know. Andrew shook his head, his lips pursed. "My bet is that it will be English," he said. "And Jane Austen is still *definitely* on the table."

*****

The kids were wired. Chaos ruled as dinner was coming to an end. All children had to be bathed and ready for bed before movie night could begin. It was one of the few times Joseph had gone willingly into the bathroom, still clutching the Blu-ray tightly in his hands.

The kitchen was tidied and the dishwashers loaded and started. Mark and Matt began the task of carrying pillows and blankets out to the garden. Adam collected a couple of wicker chairs from the patio for his grandparents and carried them to the lawn, Maureen advising him when he got too close to the bushes....or the gate...or any of the flowers. Safely arranged at the side of the lawn, Peter and Maureen settled in with an iced tea and a folded blanket to use if it became chilly.

If you were going to sit in a chair, it had to be positioned off to the side of the lawn so that those lounging on blankets and pillows wouldn't have their view obstructed. Sophia and Nic, too pregnant to sit on the ground for very long, opted for chairs, along with Matt and Janie, but everyone else brought bundles out with them to spread on the grass and make themselves comfortable.

At the rear of the garden, a small wooden fence separated the lawn from the herb garden and Adam decided it would make a great back rest, so he pulled a couple of cushions from the sofa in the pool house and arranged a comfy little spot that he graciously offered to share with Shelby. She accepted and settled in next to him with a bowl of popcorn, a bag of M & M's and two cans of Coca Cola.

"We make the perfect pair," Adam grinned. "I claimed our spot and you provide the refreshments."

"This is quite comfortable," Shelby admitted, as she sat on the quilt Adam had laid down and settled back against the pillow.

"Your comfort is my number one priority," he smiled,

and meant every word.

As everyone knew he would, Joseph won the right to pick the movie. Cars, it would be. Even though Isabelle and Amanda all but cried because they wouldn't be watching Tangled, once the movie began, everyone settled in for an exhilarating race with Lightning McQueen and Flo, Mater and the rest of the gang.

The sky shone brightly with billions of stars overhead and in the dark of night, children fell asleep one by one, heads resting on dads' laps wrapped in blankets. As the ending credits began to roll, parents whispered to each other as sleeping babies were to be carried into the house and put to bed.

Shelby watched as husbands and wives sent silent communication back and forth to each other as children were gently lifted into loving arms and carefully moved from the garden into their beds. The scene was brilliantly choreographed, with each father moving gracefully through the gate without any traffic jams and not one child stirred from their peaceful slumber. There rose in her an odd wistfulness. If she wasn't careful, the impregnable barrier she'd built around her heart would be at risk. The stirrings in the depth of her soul…the beginnings of envy she felt as she watched the blissfully happy little families all around her were threatening her peaceful existence.

It's not that she didn't want a family, she just couldn't risk screwing it up, and she was sure she would. How could she not? Her destiny was to be alone. It as the safest way to be. Yet, the picture in front of her made her heart feel a yearning she had held at bay…'til this very moment.

*****

"Eat Pray Love," Rory announced once all the children were in the house.

"No," was the consensus of the group. Not even the women wanted to watch it.

"Fine," he muttered. "We can watch my number two pick, but I am not compromising any further!" He messed around with the laptop hooked up to the projector and the screen exploded with color as the movie began. The red velvet curtains instantly gave it away.

"I love this movie!" Shelby declared.

"Me, too!" exclaimed Sophia.

"What is it?" asked Katy.

"Only one of the best films ever made," Rory explained. "Nicole Kidman and Ewan MacGregor...two of the best actors of our generation!"

"Star Wars?" asked Mark.

Beth all but fell off her chair laughing. "No, silly. It's Moulin Rouge!"

"A chick flick," Matt groaned.

"I'll give it ten minutes and then I'm going to bed," Peter grumbled.

"Hey. I'll sit through it if it means my wife is in a generous mood when it's over," David grinned and kissed Lindsey on the cheek.

"Shhhhh," Rory hissed. "It's starting."

As promised, fifteen minutes into the movie, Peter and Maureen announced they were retiring for the evening. They were not enjoying the movie and it was after their bedtime anyway. Tim helped them through the dark 'til they were safely in the house and then returned to snuggle with his wife. When Rory paused the movie thirty minutes in, because he needed to use the bathroom, Derek and Tyler stood and said they'd decided to head into town.

"There's gotta be a club or somewhere we can go," Tyler yawned, obviously bored with the movie selection.

"Anybody wanna join us?" Derek asked, looking right at Adam.

"I will!" Alex accepted the offer.

"You certainly will not!" Ben exclaimed.

"Aw, come on, Ben. Please?"

"No!" His voice told Alex there would be no more discussion.

"I'm gonna go and play a video game then," he pouted.

"Fine," Ben said, hiding a grin from his step-son.

"You wanna go?" Tyler asked Shelby.

"No, thanks. I'm gonna stay and watch the movie."

"Me, too," added Adam.

Derek smiled, a knowing smile and gave Adam the slightest of nods. The two men said goodnight and left the garden. As Rory returned from the house, he brought a bucket with cans of assorted beverages for everyone and settled back down at Andrew's side and the movie continued.

But over the course of the next hour, silently, several couples left the lawn, Matt and Janie the first to tiptoe out of the garden and up to their bedroom, hand in hand. Tim and Beth left next, with Ben and Sophia closely behind them.

As the hour got later, a slight chill was in the air and Shelby was grateful that Adam had brought an extra blanket, as she wore just shorts and a tank top. She grabbed it at the corner and pulled it across her legs.

"Cold?" Adam whispered. She nodded. He scooted a little closer, wrapped his arm around her and pulled the blanket over both of them, giving her the warmth of the quilt and his body. It felt so natural to have her in his arms. He knew it was where she belonged. Within minutes he heard her steady, deep breathing and realized she'd fallen asleep. Content, Adam watched the movie with a smile.

Even the intense critique of the film by Mark and Katy as the credits rolled didn't wake Shelby. She was curled into Adam's side and out for the count. As several members of the family offered their assistance to help him get her up to her room, Adam shook his head and shooed them away, leaving them in the garden alone.

He kissed her on the top of her head, enjoying the sweet smell of her shampoo and tilted his head back and gazed at the stars. Her head rested on his chest, over his heart, his arm wrapped around her protectively, his hand resting on her hip. He could stay like this forever, with the woman he loved at his side.

He ran his fingers through her hair and pulled the blanket over her shoulder. The he settled back, closed his eyes and drifted off to sleep.

*****

The sun rose early and with it, the birds. Chirping happily high in the trees, Adam's eyes fluttered open, grateful for the bush next to the house that was giving his eyes some relief from the bright sun glaring down on him. At some point, he'd kicked off the blanket, the morning dawning warm.

However, Shelby was no longer curled beside him. She was nowhere to be seen. Rubbing his neck and stretching his back, Adam scrambled to his feet and yawned. He picked up the pillows and blankets and walked to the pool house. There wasn't a sound coming from the house. It was still very early.

Falling onto the bed, Adam closed his eyes and quickly fell asleep.

*****

Shelby watched Adam shuffle into the pool house, still half asleep, from behind the curtain in the great room. She'd awoken just a few minutes earlier to find her hand caressing his chest. It had felt wonderful and had scared her wide awake.

The last few days had sent her into an emotional tailspin and every time she attempted to check herself, there was something else that unbalanced her...made her question the decisions that had managed to keep her sane all these years.

Being held by Adam had given her an overwhelming sense of calm and safety...something she sorely lacked most of the time. Yet, she'd slept more deeply in his arms than any time in the last twelve years, and her dreams didn't wake her in a panicked sweat.

She'd already acknowledged her feelings for him. And he'd certainly left no doubt as to how he felt about her. However, that wasn't enough for her to allow the protective walls she'd spent years erecting be torn apart, leaving her vulnerable.

But it was Adam...and Adam would *never* hurt her, of that she was sure.

The voices behind her had her turning around to see Mark and Katy bouncing down the stairs. They were dressed for a run.

"Morning," Katy smiled. "You're up early."

Shelby returned the smile. "Just beat you. I'm gonna make coffee. Want some?"

Mark shook his head. "No thanks. We're off for a run on the beach. Wanna join us?"

Shelby chuckled. "How many times have you asked me to join you on a run? And how many times have I accepted?"

Mark grinned.

"That's right," she continued. "None!" she laughed. "Enjoy the beach." She watched as they left the house, hand in hand, and walked down to the hard sand by the water and stretched before taking off at a leisurely pace.

She'd phoned Katy many times after her move to Wisconsin to live with her grandmother. Katy had been the one who'd understood what she was feeling and had let her talk with never a judgment, only love and support in return. Without Katy, Shelby didn't want to think about what her life might have been like. Katy, and Mark, had loved her unconditionally and had been there for her every moment of her life since that day when she landed in Katy's Emergency Room back in Portland, twelve long years ago. They'd become the parents she'd never had. They had become her family. The whole Lathem clan was her family and she loved them all.

She would wait for Katy to return. Once again, she needed to talk and she knew that Katy would gladly listen.

21.

Clarity

Tyler said goodbye to his parents and grandparents and loaded his suitcase into the trunk of the Jeep and climbed into the passenger's seat, with Adam behind the wheel. His vacation was over. A pressing business matter had him returning to New York a few days early and Adam had offered to drive him to the airport. As the car drove away, Peter and Maureen returned to the house and Matt and Janie, along with Ella and Christopher, headed to the beach. Shelby sat by the pool, waiting for a glimpse of Katy and Mark returning from their morning run.

She watched their tiny figures get bigger and bigger as they got closer and closer to the house. They stopped a couple of hundred yards away and stretched their warm and tired muscles, then walked hand in hand towards the house, stopping just beyond the trail, under a palm tree. Mark leaned his back against the trunk and pulled Katy into his arms and kissed her…thoroughly. He held her head gently in his hands and Katy pressed her body against his. Shelby wondered if she should look away, but couldn't seem to tear her gaze from the lovers. It was clear to anyone who'd seen them that they had eyes only for each another, that their hearts and souls were eternally joined. Love could be a beautiful thing. Mark and Katy were absolute proof of that.

A lone tear escaped Shelby's eye. Wiping it away quickly, she wrestled with her raging emotions and the desire to know what it felt like to be passionately loved. The words from the movie the night before, to love and to be loved in return, swirled through her mind. A desperate longing swelled inside her as she watched the kiss finally come to an end, Mark and Katy with a special smile for the other and then taking her once again by the hand, Mark leading her to the gate and up the trail to the house.

"When you have some spare time, could I talk to you?" Shelby asked as they walked to the house.

"Of course," Katy smiled. "Why don't you give me an hour? I'll shower and then let's go into town and have lunch…just the two of us."

"Sounds great," Shelby nodded. "Thanks."

"Can I come?" Mark asked.

"No!" Katy laughed. "Girl time!"

Shelby chuckled as Mark pretended to pout, Katy slapping him playfully on the arm.

"I'll meet you down here. One hour," Katy smiled as she entered the house.

*****

"Iced tea, please," Katy asked the waitress.

"I'll just have water with lemon, please," smiled Shelby.

"So," Katy asked, "I'm assuming this has to do with Adam?"

Shelby's eyes almost popped out of her head. "How…why…but I never…"

"Aw, honey," Katy interrupted. "Just tell me."

"You never like the small talk, do you? Right to the point."

"It saves so much time. Plus, I hate all the bullshit," she grinned.

"He told me was in love in me," Shelby blurted it out.

"Of course he is!"

"Why do you say that? How on earth would you know that?" Shelby asked, perplexed by the quick response.

"I've seen the way he looks at you…and I've seen the way you are with him. This is no great revelation."

"Really?"

"Really," Katy nodded.

"So then what do I do?"

Katy chuckled. "What do you want to do?"

"I don't know," Shelby admitted.

"Yes, you do."

Looking up at the waitress as she delivered their drinks, Shelby took the quiet moment to take a breath.

Could she really admit to Katy, and to herself, what she really, *really* wanted?

Katy could almost read her thoughts. "Honey, I know what you had to do to survive all those years ago and you were totally justified in cutting yourself off from men, at keeping them all at a safe distance. And you have given yourself time to heal and to mature and to get your life together and work hard to start your career. I would never tell you that your choices were wrong. Nobody would! You are amazing! You're my hero! I look at you and am reminded at the strength of the human spirit. You haven't let your past define your future, well, until this very moment. What you do today will determine how you choose to spend the rest of your life. Do you allow love into your life, or will you remain alone?"

Shelby took a deep breath but didn't speak.

"There are lots of people who are perfectly content to be alone, and I'm not going to judge their choices. But I know you, Shelby, and I see how you are when you're with Adam. Your whole being lights up, your eyes reflect the happiness you feel inside. I don't know if you're consciously aware of it, but you do. It has a name."

"I'm in love with him," Shelby whispered.

Katy smiled, knowing how much Shelby risked by admitting her feelings. "Yes, you are, and have been for quite some time. The question is, will you let it guide you now, or will you bury it deep and never realize the true joy a healthy relationship?"

The waitress returned for their orders, giving Shelby time to digest the words of the woman she loved like a mother.

As though, once again, reading her thoughts, Katy, after placing her order, reached across the table and took Shelby's hand in hers. "I know I'm not your mother, but I love you like a daughter, and I only want to see you gloriously happy. You deserve to be."

With everything in her mind coming together like a puzzle, piece by piece being linked to form the picture she'd long ago accepted she'd never have, Shelby was surprised to see that she had, in fact, had all along the things she'd been denied as a child – a mother, a father, and a family.

For the second time that day, another tear escaped and ran down her cheek.

"Honey, what's wrong?" Katy's concern obvious in her voice.

Shelby shook her head, unable to speak for a moment. When she finally formed the words, her voice cracked as she sputtered, "I love you like a mother. You've been my mother for all these years and…and you *are* my mother."

Jumping from her chair, Katy ran around the table and embraced Shelby, holding her tightly in her arms and letting her cry 'til she was able to compose herself. Diners at nearby tables stared and whispered, but the two women were oblivious to it all, only focusing on the moment, on the bond they shared and were just now realizing how strong and permanent it really was.

"You don't need to deny yourself anything, Shelby. You can have whatever you want. Just reach for it and take it."

"It sounds so easy," Shelby sniffed.

Katy chuckled. "That's deceiving. It actually isn't easy at all! It takes a great deal of courage to take control of your life and future. And if I know anything it's that you are one of the most courageous people I have ever met. But I'm here for you…Mark, too. We love you and want to see you happy."

"I know," Shelby nodded.

"You're the one who has to decide how to live your life and if you want to share it with someone special."

"He is someone special. I realize now that he's been by my side for all these years and I just took it for granted, not appreciating him at all."

"No," Katy said. "You've appreciated everything about him. You've just been too scared to see that there is a future for you with him. He is a good man, honey. I've known Adam since the day he was born. I watched him take his first steps and I was there when he graduated from college. He is the kind of man I would want my daughter to fall in love with. He is the kind of man I would *trust* my daughter with."

"I'm just not sure that…that I know how to…to be in love."

"Yes you do. And if you really are unsure? Let Adam guide you."

Salads were delivered and glasses refilled. The

conversation switched, gradually, to Shelby's residency and the exciting opportunities that awaited her at Mount Sinai Hospital, until the plates were cleared and the check was paid. The drive home was peaceful and Shelby gathered her thoughts, deciding what her next step should be. Could she just reach for it? Was that all there was to it?

*****

There were just two more days 'til the Lathems left the beautiful island of Grand Bahama and fly back to the concrete jungle that was New York City. There seemed to be a cloud hanging over the adults, knowing that the peaceful relaxation time was coming to an end, that reality was waiting for them back at home. The children, however, were oblivious and wanted to play in the pool, so the majority of the family were outside on the patio when Shelby and Katy arrived home.

"Good lunch?" Mark asked as he stood to welcome his wife home with a kiss.

"Yes," Shelby smiled. "A good lunch."

"I'll go get changed," Katy said. "Then we can swim." The two women headed inside and up to their rooms.

Adam watched Shelby. There was something different about her…something he couldn't put his finger on, but different nevertheless. He anxiously awaited her return. Which turned out to be almost half an hour. Katy was down and in the pool playing with her nieces and nephews in ten, but Shelby made him wait.

And it was worth it. She exited the house wearing the new bikini she'd found in Freeport, along with a sarong in the same coral shades made of silk and tied low on her hips. Adam almost swallowed his tongue.

"Look at you!" Paul grinned. "Damn!"

"You make those Victoria Secret models look like chubby, dumpy trolls," Sophia said.

"I don't think so," Shelby blushed.

"Uh, yeah, you do," Beth added.

"You need one of those," Tim said to Beth, nodding at Shelby's swim suit.

"I'll be able to wear it for the next two weeks, and then...well, then I'll look like Shamu."

"A beautiful Shamu, though," Tim grinned.

Shelby dropped her towel on the empty chair next to Janie and sat down, slipping of her flip flops and lounging back in the sun. Janie was watching Adam, and his reaction to the skimpy bits of triangle shaped fabric that covered a very small portion of Shelby's hourglass shape. It appeared he'd forgotten how to breathe.

"Adam," she called, snapping him out of the trance he was in. "Would you please get some bottles of water from the fridge?"

"Uh, sure," he nodded. He stood and walked to the glass doors of the house, not taking his eyes of her until he was inside.

The rest of the afternoon passed pleasantly enjoying

the pool and the sun and spending time together as family. When Cynthia announced fresh baked cookies and milkshakes were available in the kitchen, the party broke up quickly, leaving an empty chair next to Shelby that Adam wasted no time in claiming.

"I'd like to ask you on an official second date," he smiled. "How about this evening?"

She didn't even have to ponder the question. "I'd like that."

*****

"We've always been able to talk honestly, right?" Shelby asked as the hostess seated them at their table.

Adam nodded. "Yes, that's one of the many things I like about you."

"Well, then this dinner may not be what you had planned, but I think there's some things we...*I* need to talk about...to say out loud...to you."

"We can talk about whatever you want. And all I had planned was you and I being together. However you decide we do that is fine with me," he winked.

Earlier, as she was showering and getting ready for their date, Shelby had decided that she needed to lay her cards out on the table, to leave nothing unsaid. If, and it was a *big* if, they stood a chance at having a relationship, he would need to understand what she was feeling and why. She only hoped it didn't scare him away. That realization had shocked her...hoping that there was indeed a future for them together. And once she had accepted it as truth, she was hopeful that her emotional wounds had finally healed, allowing her to move on and find a peace her life had been missing…that part that would make her feel whole.

"Good," she smiled. "I hope you still think that at the end of the evening."

Adam chuckled. "There's nothing that you can say to me that will scare me away, or shock me enough to retract any declaration of love for you."

After ordering, Shelby took a deep breath, clasped her hands in her lap and looked up at Adam who was studying her, his head slightly tilted.

"Just tell me what you need to say," he encouraged.

"Okay," she nodded. "You know that my childhood was…was less than idyllic. I was pretty much left to fend for myself for as long as I can remember, at least the memories I haven't blocked out," she added. "The only normalcy I had was when I was at school. That may be one reason I value education. I don't know, but I do now that home was hell."

"I know," Adam said. "I can't even imagine."

"I watch Ella cooking with her mom or with Cynthia and I'm reminded that I never did that. I rarely had cooked meals…only at school. And sitting on the floor playing board games? Never. Although I remember having a deck of cards and playing with them like dolls. There was a mommy and a daddy and I remember sitting playing with them for hours. But not quite the same as Legos, or Candy Land, is it?"

"I'm sorry," Adam said as his heart broke for her.

"It's all in the past," she shrugged.

"Is it? Really?"

"The physical scars have healed," she continued, unconsciously laying her hand over her tummy, the scar covered by her skirt. "But the emotional ones? Well, I wondered if I would ever be normal."

Adam shook his head. "You are normal and..."

"No, it's okay," Shelby interrupted. "I'm not. How could I be? But I've come to terms with that and I'm okay with it. Anyway, normal is overrated," she smiled. "But for all these years I've told myself that I can't have a normal, healthy relationship because I wouldn't even know how to have one...what it even looks like. But I realized today that that was just a lie I told myself to keep others at a safe distance. I have beautiful examples of what a healthy relationship looks like. I have Mark and Katy, and Matt and your mom, and Peter and Maureen, and all the other marriages in this family. I see you and your mom's relationship and Katy and Derek's and it finally clicked for me today that I have that with Katy and Mark. For almost half my life they have been the parental figures that have loved me unconditionally and I love them right back. I said I didn't have a maternal role model. I've told myself that over and over again and that's a lie. A big fat lie. I do! I have my grandmother. I have Katy. I have Janie and Maureen. I have so many of them that I didn't even recognize what was right in front of me."

"So, what are you saying?"

"That while I have no clue what the future holds for me, I shouldn't rule out anything. I don't want to limit my opportunities because I'm afraid. I don't want to lose out on love because I didn't think I deserved it."

"Oh, Shelby! You deserve everything in this world that's good and beautiful because *you* are good and beautiful. I love you…with all that I am."

"I know," she smiled. "And I am extremely grateful."

"Grateful?" Adam didn't like the sound of that…or the "*but*" he heard in her voice.

"Yes, grateful. Without you telling me that you loved me, I wouldn't have taken this emotional journey the past couple of days and realized, with a clarity I'm not sure I even appreciate, how I truly feel. And for that, I am grateful."

He attempted a smile, but failed. The waitress delivered their entrees and they both picked up a knife and fork, Adam pausing to say, "But?"

"But what?"

"You're grateful, but," he said.

"There is no but," she smiled. "I love you, too."

*****

Adam ate quickly and asked for the check, leaving Shelby to either leave what was still on her plate uneaten or ask for a box. She decided to just leave it.

They drove home, the windows down, allowing the cool sea breeze to swirl through their hair. Adam reached for her hand placed gently in her lap and squeezed it, not wanting to ruin the moment with a trite expression that he knew would just sound cheesy. Instead, he kept his eyes on the road and drove them home safely.

Once the car was locked in the garage, Adam led her by the hand past the house to the water. The sun was setting behind them and the beach was deserted. "Let's walk," he whispered.

Leaving their shoes at the gate, they wandered barefoot over the soft sand, fingers entwined, listening to the sea gently lapping at their feet.

"I wish I could eloquently state what I'm feeling right now," he admitted. "But I can't find words to describe it."

"Gregory likes to build forts in the sand," Shelby said. "He spends hours making walls and motes and tunnels and then, after all the work has been done, he crushes them with buckets of water. I kind of feel like that fort right now."

"And that's a good thing?"

"A very good thing," Shelby smiled. "I've spent all of my life building these impenetrable walls to protect myself from the things I want most, because I'm afraid. And you came in with buckets of water and blew them to smithereens. I feel free! For the first time I can remember, I feel free."

Adam pulled her into his arms and swung her around, her feet lifting from the ground and she giggled as he twirled her under the stars. As her feet found the ground once more, and their movement stopped, Adam's grip tightened and he lowered his head to hers, covering her mouth with his.

He felt her flinch but didn't release his hold. He kissed her gently and he felt her shoulders eventually relax, her hands cautiously lay on his hips. His tongue barely grazed her lip and once again she tensed, but eased as she accepted him. In minutes, he was inside her mouth, his tongue tasting her, sliding over her smooth straight teeth and dancing with her tongue as she experienced how truly divine a great kiss could be.

Pulling back, gasping for air, she lay her head on his chest and gripped him tightly around the waist. "Wow," she whispered.

"Double wow," he said into her hair as he fought for control of his body.

"I need you to go slow. There are…are demons I have when it comes to…to this."

Adam understood and he wished he could take those memories from her. But he hoped that by giving her good memories, memories of him worshipping her body, those demons would become a thing of the past. "We'll go as slow as you need. I'll never hurt you. I promise. I'd rather die than hurt you." He held her snugly to his body, never willing to ever let her go.

22.

Desire

Her pulse quickened and her breathing was shallow. She stood in the middle of the room as Adam locked the door and closed the curtains in the pool house. He clicked on the lamp beside the bed and then came and stood directly in front of her, pushing a stray piece of hair behind her ear.

"Don't be nervous, Shelby. We won't do anything that makes you uncomfortable. We have all the time in the world. Just knowing you love me is all I need."

She looked up at him, her eyes big and bright, with a look of relief, perhaps. "It's not that I don't want to…to try, it's just…" Her voice trailed off.

"Hey, it's okay." He held her face gently in his hands. "No pressure. Slow and easy. And, if you never want me to touch me, I'll abide by that, too. I promise you, Shelby, I'll never hurt you. Never! Why don't we just cuddle and watch some TV?"

Shelby nodded as Adam pushed the bed pillows up against the bed head and pulled back the comforter. He slipped out of his flip flops and took his wallet from the pocket of his shorts and removed his watch from his wrist. He climbed onto the bed, leaning back on the fluffy pillows and motioned for her to join him, to which she quickly complied. Settling in next to him, she laid her head on his chest, her hand resting on his abdomen as Adam clicked on the television and after flicking through several channels, settled on a classic...an episode of Friends.

However, neither of them were watching. Adam caressed her back and stroked her long golden hair. Shelby listened to the steady beating of his heart and wondered what if would be like to not be afraid of physical intimacy...of what they would be doing if she wasn't so terrified. She loved him and wanted to show him but didn't know how. Adam more than sensed her hesitation and uncertainty. He felt it. And he knew that if their relationship stood a chance of lasting, it was dependent upon his sensitivity to her needs.

The next episode of the sitcom began, Adam still lightly touching her in a non-sexual way, giving her time to adjust to him being so close. Everything that would happen would be a first for her and he didn't want there to be any regrets, for either of them. It would devastate him if he hurt her, physically or emotionally. This was the woman he wanted to spend the rest of his life with. He wasn't going to screw it up.

At the first set of commercials, Shelby spoke quietly. "I'm not watching it if you want to just turn it off."

"Why don't we just go to sleep, then?" he asked. "It's late."

Shelby nodded so Adam found the remote and turned the television off. Scooting down the bed, he kept his arm around her, holding her close, and reached for the switch on the lamp. He felt her head move, now looking up at him through the darkness. Her hand touched his cheek and he bent down to her 'til his lips found hers, warm and moist...inviting. He kissed her gently, but his desire was so strong it was difficult to maintain the self-control necessary.

But she surprised him by opening her mouth to him and slipped her tongue into his, tentatively exploring the feel of him. Keenly aware of his arousal, he kept his hands on her back, rigid and still. Her tongue grazing over his teeth, finding his tongue and innocently discovering the pleasures of a simple kiss, made his blood boil.

"I like this," she whispered, as she pulled away.

"Me, too," he replied.

"Can we kiss some more?"

He smiled. "Absolutely." And he pulled her up and on top of him, giving her all of the control. She took it readily and placed her lips on his and kissed him as lovers would. He held her head in his hands and when her hips moved he let go and grabbed the pillows at his head.

"What's wrong?" she asked. "Are you alright?" As she pushed herself up on her hands and looked at him, the pressure from her hips had him squirming a little more.

"Ah, just a little turned on and every time you move like that," he said as she wriggled again, "I am having to try and think of my mom and other stuff that works the same way as a cold shower would."

"Oh, sorry."

"Don't be sorry," he grinned. "You feel good. Just a little *too* good."

"You feel good, too. And, maybe, we don't have to go quite as slow."

He exhaled. "But you'll tell me if you need me to stop?"

She nodded. "I will." Shelby knew that this was the moment Katy had spoken of. This was the moment that would change the course of her future and while petrified, she was certain of her decision, digging deep to the find the courage to choose her future.

He'd waited for years to love her. Clicking the lamp back on, he wanted to see her as he undressed her, and he wanted her to see him. They each knelt on the bed, facing each other, and Adam unbuttoned his shirt and threw it on the floor then pulled her tank top over her head and discarded it the same way. She sat in her bra, her soft golden skin peeking through the delicate white lace. Ever so slightly, his finger traced over her lush mounds of flesh until he stopped at the hook nestled in her cleavage.

Their eyes met, the question hanging in the air. Taking a deep breath, she nodded and looked down at his hand. With a quick flick, the hook popped open and gently he pulled the straps down her arms. The rosy buds called to him like a siren and he lowered his head and took each one into his mouth, sucking gently. He heard her gasp, felt her back arch to him and smiled. Knowing she was enjoying it as much as he, Adam nipped with his teeth and rolled his tongue over and over her distended nipples as he lowered her down onto her back.

With her fingers in his hair, she held him to her breasts, writhing underneath him as he worshipped her body with his mouth.

"Oh, Adam," she whimpered.

He pulled away and rolled back onto his ankles. "I'm going to take off your skirt, 'k?"

She nodded, her eyes still tightly closed. Rolling her onto her side, he made quick work of the button and zipper at her back. It was discarded on the floor to join the other articles of clothes. All that remained was her panties, white lace that matched her bra. Kissing the inside of her thigh made her flinch, eyelids shooting open and pushing herself up on her elbows, fear in her eyes.

"I'm not gonna hurt you. Let me love you. Let me show how good it's gonna be," he soothed.

Taking a deep breath, she fell back to the bed, her complete trust in him touching him to the core...his soul. He kissed her again, his hands caressing the silky smooth skin of her legs. Her musky scent filled him and as he moved higher his need for her was overwhelming. His hand lightly brushed over her panties, wet with excitement and the pulsing in his groin quickened. He licked the lace and she cried out his name once more. She needed his loving as much he needed to love her.

He removed her panties and spread her legs wide, kneeling between them and burying his face in the curly hair that covered her. Every one of his senses were on overload as he looked up to see her nipples protruding and hard, her mouth open begging for breath, eyes squeezed shut. Her breath was shallow and he felt her pulse under his lips. Parting her with his tongue she again cried his name and he knew it was just a matter of moments before she would shatter under his touch.

Licking and tasting her almost sent him over the edge but he willed himself to hold on as he brought her to the peak and as her body froze, she arched her back and a violent spasm held her as she cried out again, delirious in the overwhelming sensation racking her entire body.

Her lifeless body lay limp and spent as Adam lay his head on her stomach. He needed a moment to conquer control before he, too, exploded. Never had taking a woman to orgasm given him such fulfillment…and such a difficulty in controlling his own needs and desires. The emotional connection he felt with Shelby was beyond words and he hoped she felt it, too.

A minute or two had passed before she spoke. "I…I…That was incredible. You…oh, boy…thank you."

Adam grinned. Speechless was good. "We aren't done yet."

"Okay." He heard the smile in her voice.

"But why don't you rest for a minute first."

"Good idea."

*****

She slept for several hours, cradled in his arms. Adam dozed but he wasn't relaxed enough to drift into a deep sleep. Oh, how he loved her. He knew without doubt that she was his future. Matt was right when he said that the Lathem men knew what they wanted and he was no exception. Shelby was who he wanted to spend the rest of his life with and he hoped…desperately hoped that he'd be able to convince her of that fact. He knew that she trusted him and it was the sweetest gift she could ever have given him. She had given herself to him willingly. But he knew it wasn't over yet. He *had* to be inside her. He needed it as much as he needed air. He didn't want to wake her but he desperately wanted to finish what they'd started.

He carefully slid from the bed and visited the bathroom, and removed his shorts and briefs while he was there. It was still dark outside. There was still lots of time. As he returned to the bed she rolled into him and said, "I had the most amazing dreams."

"Me, too," he grinned. "Only mine was real."

"Thank you," she whispered.

"The best is yet to come."

"Really? I'm not sure I believe you."

"Let me prove it to you."

Adam rolled on top of her, covering her with his body. He kissed her and she responded immediately. His hips pushed into hers, his erection pressing into her. She responded and lifted her hips to his, silently consenting to what was about to happen. There wouldn't be a lot of time for foreplay…his control was coming to an end.

With his knees, he parted her legs and settled between them, poised at her entrance. The moment he felt her hips roll underneath him, he plunged inside her and stilled. She stiffened, her eyelids flying open, an instant terror in her eyes.

"I love you, Shelby," he declared again. "I will never hurt you. Trust me."

She took a deep breath and exhaled slowly. He felt her muscles relax, one by one, and the fear that was so evident, slowly faded away. "I trust you," she whispered. "With my life and my heart."

Kissing her again, this time gently, she snaked her arms around his neck and held their bodies together. He felt a tear on his thumb as he caressed her cheek.

"Don't cry," he pleaded.

"I've always known that sex was bad…that men could be so cruel…but now…," she sobbed.

"This isn't just sex. This is making love. I love you. Please don't cry."

"I love you, Adam. Thank you for not giving up on me."

*****

The morning sun shone through the tiny slits in the curtains. Shelby and Adam were entwined, clinging to each other in a deep sleep. They'd made love twice, the second time with no memories of the past haunting her…the demons no longer stalking her…her dreams now of Adam and their future together.

As they awoke to the sounds of splashing in the pool, Shelby looked at the clock. It was after ten.

"I don't care what time it is," Adam growled, his eyes

still closed. "You aren't going anywhere." He pulled her tighter.

"People are going to wonder…"

"I don't care," he grumbled. "I've got you naked in my bed and I'm not letting you go…ever!"

Shelby laughed. "At some point, we're going to have to leave the pool house. If nothing else, we have to get on a plane tomorrow and go home."

"We can deal with that tomorrow."

"What a trip this has been."

Adam agreed. "So much has happened in just a couple of weeks."

"It'll probably be good to get back to normal."

"I don't want things to go back to the way they were," he said as he sat up straight.

"Well," Shelby said, "There's work and stuff and…"

"I know but I've waited for you for a long time and I'm not going back to the old status quo. I want you by my side…always."

"So, are you talking about moving in together?" she asked.

"No, I'm not."

"Oh," Shelby said, surprising herself as she heard the slight disappointment in her reply.

"Will you marry me? Will you be Mrs. Dr. Adam Anderson? Or Dr. Shelby Anderson? I kind of like that better," he grinned.

"Marry you?" her eyes were open wide. "This is a bit sudden, isn't it?"

"Not for me!" he chuckled. "I've been in love with you for years, just waiting for you. Marry me," he nodded.

*****

"She's not in her room," Katy said. "It appears her bed wasn't slept in."

"The car is in the garage so I know they came back from town last night," Janie added.

"Maybe we should check the pool house to see if Adam is there," Katy suggested.

"No!" Mark exclaimed. "Leave them alone!"

"So they're there? Together?" Janie asked.

"It doesn't matter if they are or not," Matt added. "Give them some privacy."

"So they *are* there?" Katy asked.

The four of them were in the library trying to decide what time to leave for New York the following day, but the whereabouts of Shelby and Adam had been the main topic of conversation.

"Now, can we talk about tomorrow?" Mark said.

"Just not too early," Janie said. "It'll take a while to get all the kids ready."

"So, eleven?" Matt asked.

"That puts us home before dinner. Perhaps the babies will sleep on the plane," Katy said.

"Okay. I'll call to confirm," Matt said as he stood and headed out of the room.

"Matt? Do you have a second?" Adam asked him in the hallway.

Noticing the grip he had on Shelby's hand, he bit his lip so as to not smile. "Sure. Privately?"

"Uh, well, is Mom around?"

"She's in the library with Mark and Katy."

"Oh, good," Shelby smiled. "We were looking for them, too."

Matt turned around and walked back to join the others, Adam and Shelby at his heels. All eyes looked up as they entered the room. Matt sat down next to his wife and waited, more interested in how his wife would react than the actual news itself, as he was pretty sure he knew what they were about to say...their faces said it all.

"We wanted to tell you guys first, and, uh, we're glad that you're all together," Adam said. "We can do this all at once."

"Tell us what?" Janie asked.

"We...Shelby and I are getting married."

Katy and Janie looked at each other and grinned. Matt and Mark both breathed a sigh of relief.

"Ah, you want to say anything?" Shelby asked.

"Congratulations," Janie smiled as she stood and hugged her son and then took Shelby into an embrace.

Katy stood and grinned. "It's about time."

Epilogue

Matt and Janie collapsed on their bed after tucking in the children after a long and eventful day.

"I'm beat!" sighed Janie. "But it was absolutely perfect, wasn't it?"

Matt rolled onto his side and kissed his wife, a long lingering kiss. "It was perfect. You and Katy are master wedding planners," he chuckled.

"Only three more to go," she grinned.

"Considering Christopher is just approaching his ninth birthday, I'd say it'll be a *long* while before they're *all* married."

Adam had married Shelby in a beautiful ceremony at St. Luke's that afternoon. Sadly, Father Todd who had performed the marriage ceremony for Matt and Janie had retired, but the young priest, Father James, had risen to the occasion, reading beautiful passages from the Bible and giving sound advice to the young couple. As they newlyweds kissed for the first time as husband and wife, both Janie and Katy looked at each other and smiled, knowing they couldn't have picked better spouses for their children.

The reception, a magical winter scene in the ballroom of The Plaza, had been beyond perfect, and the bride looked stunning in her beaded Vera Wang gown and Adam had rivaled Prince Charming in his black Armani tuxedo. They only had eyes for each other and probably didn't even notice the months of planning and impeccable execution that had taken place to make their day one to remember. But Janie didn't mind. Just seeing them so happy and blissfully in love with each other had made it all worth it.

The whole family had been there, including the two newest additions, Ben and Sophia's little one, Raymond Aldo Lathem, and Paul and Nic's baby girl, born just four days later, Sarah Nicole. They'd both managed to sleep through most of the day.

Beth had needed to leave the party early. The triplets were due in just two months and the doctors were extremely concerned she could go into labor at any time, so her appearance was short, but managed to stand for all for the family pictures with Tim constantly at her side for emotional, and physical, support.

Janie kicked off her shoes and slid into Matt's arms. "I'll sleep well tonight," she sighed.

"You most certainly will," he chuckled as he pulled her close and kissed her with a kiss that curled her toes.

*****

Adam and Shelby returned to the Lathem estate in the Bahamas for their honeymoon. The first night was spent in the pool house, a quiet night, full of firsts as husband and wife, just as it had been a few months earlier.

"I love you, Mrs. Anderson," he whispered in her ear.

"Mmm. I like the sound of that, Mr. Anderson," she smiled.

"Me, too. But no more talking," he said and kissed her.

*****

The delivery driver took the clipboard from Maureen's hands once she'd signed it and handed her the large package. Already knowing what it was, she excitedly returned to the living room and yelled for Peter to join her as she unwrapped the picture from the brown paper.

Sitting beside each other, they looked at the beautifully framed photograph in front of them. It was the latest family picture, taken just a few weeks earlier at Adam and Shelby's wedding. Their entire family was there; seven sons, six daughters-in-law, one son-in-law and seventeen grandchildren. Since the photo had been taken, Beth had given birth to the triplets, who were now home after spending two weeks in the NICU, bringing the total of grandchildren to twenty.

Peter chuckled. "We made a fine looking family."

"Didn't we?" Maureen agreed with a big smile. "We're very blessed."

"Yes…we are."

THE END

Please visit the First Class Novels website where you can subscribe to receive elite notifications about upcoming new releases, news and events.

Join the conversation on our blog and let us know what you love about First Class Novels.

http://www.firstclassnovels.com

About the Author

AJ Harmon was born and raised in Perth, Western Australia. She currently resides in Oregon, USA, with her husband Brad. They have two grown children, her pride and joy, and a dog named Max.

An avid reader of the Romance genre, the books in her personal library range from historical to erotica and everything in between. "I love reading a sweet romance set in the English Regency period where men were gentlemen and the women pretended to be naïve. But sometimes you just need a hot sexy romance to cap off a long week," she smiled. The bookshelves in her home are filled with a variety of authors and she is humbled to now be among their ranks.

AJ is a new author, finding her passion in writing after her children had left home, leaving her and her husband empty-nesters. She says the 'First Class' series has been a pleasure for her to write and has been absolutely delightful that readers have received them with such a warm embrace. "It will be hard to say goodbye to the Lathems," she said. "They have become a huge part of my life and I consider them my family." The series has nine volumes in total and AJ considers it to be one of her greatest achievements. "This series has changed my life and the readers have brought me more love and joy than I ever hoped for. My life is a fairytale."

AJ is excited to begin work on her next project, a new series coming in 2014.

Made in the USA
Charleston, SC
08 December 2013